PURSUIT
in the
French Alps

BY PAUL-JACQUES BONZON

illustrated by Margery Gill

American Education Publications/A Xerox Company
Middletown, Connecticut

Contents

1

Wolf Ridge

WINTER had been mild that year in the French Alps, and spring came earlier than usual. It was only the middle of May, but already the snow, eaten away by the sun, was retreating up the mountain slopes, uncovering fresh new grass that grew greener each day. The cattle were being driven up for pasture, and it was time to think of the first crop of hay in the heights.

Early one morning, just as the sun was beginning to lean over the mountains, Vincent left Lauzière, his village, on mule-back. He whistled joyously, glad to be setting out for the hut on Wolf Ridge. There he would stay alone for two, maybe three months, cutting hay in the high mountain pastures.

It would be Vincent's first summer on his own in the heights. Every other year he had gone up with his mother and father and little brother, Bernard. But during the previous winter, his father had suffered a bad fall in the Low Dale, and scything hay was still too strenuous for him. His mother had thought of going up to the hut in his place, but scything hay was no work for a woman. Besides, her family needed her at home.

While his parents were debating the problem a few days before, Vincent had found the courage to make his suggestion. "Why not let me go up to Wolf Ridge? I'm not afraid of work—I'm strong as a horse—and I'd love to go up to the hut."

At first his mother had protested—he didn't know how lonely it would be up in the mountains by himself; he had his school year to finish; and besides, he was too young. Although Vincent was a tall and husky fourteen, his mother still thought of him as a little boy.

"I'm sure the schoolmaster will let me go," Vincent had argued. "Don't worry, Mother. I won't be scared alone up there. And anyway, I'll be coming down for supplies every week."

But it was his father who had finally persuaded her to agree to the idea. "After all, why shouldn't Vincent go? He's not a child anymore."

His father found him fit to do a man's work. Nothing he could have said would have pleased Vincent more.

Now the boy urged Bichounette, his mule, up along the trail leading to the heights. Below, in the valley, he always felt crushed beneath the mountains. Above, at an altitude of more

than four thousand five hundred feet, the sky would seem ten times larger, and all the Alps would be spread out for him.

Two big bags were wedged against his thighs, containing supplies for the week: a round loaf of bread with a hole in the middle, like a doughnut, so it would not grow stale as quickly as other sorts; potatoes, noodles, and cheese. They also contained tools, and books the schoolmaster had lent him to read of an evening as he sat by his stove. Vincent had promised the schoolmaster that he would study them in return for permission to leave his classes early.

Bichounette was a sturdy beast, accustomed to heavy work in the mountains, but she was bowed down by this load, and beginning to breathe hard.

So that she could get her wind, Vincent stopped and dismounted in a clearing in a little firwood where the trees stood straight as candles. He sat on the grass and gazed down on his village, already in shadow. How tiny it looked, just a few houses scattered round the Servette, that rushing torrent of gray snow water whose roar still reached him. Slowly his eyes traveled along the narrow valley, and lifted toward the mountaintops, still covered with great blankets of snow and ice. He knew them all by name: the Needle of Paradise, the jagged peak of Roquebrune, and in the distance the tip of the Dard. Nearly all of them were over nine thousand feet, and on the other side, as an eagle flies, was Italy.

"Italy!" Vincent said aloud. Just the name possessed a magic and excitement for him; he had never been in Italy.

A high white barrier stood between the two countries, and the people of Lauzière rarely traveled through Young Deer Pass, which was blocked by snow for more than six months of the year. To Vincent it looked like a narrow groove carved in the living rock, and he remembered the stories told about it in Lauzière, and how it had taken its name from the chamois and ibex that leapt from one side to the other whenever they migrated.

He set off again as soon as Bichounette had got her wind back. The air grew lighter and more transparent as he climbed, so that he had to breathe deeply, with a delightful sensation of well-being.

All at once the hut came into view, set upon a sort of grassy spur that everyone called Wolf Ridge, though no one knew why. It was a big cabin, rather than a hut, with a huge hayloft above, strongly built to resist storm and wind. And that was where Vincent was going to live for the next two months, maybe longer, entirely alone. But he had not climbed up to Wolf Ridge to sleep in the sun among the sweet-scented mountain plants. There was hard work to be done. From dawn to dusk he would be cutting the sweet-smelling grass with wide sweeps of his scythe, on slopes so steep there was always danger he might fall into the ravine if he were not careful. Then later he must bring the hay down on the sledge, and store it to feed to the cattle through the long winter. But he was young and strong, and the thought of such heavy labor did not alarm him.

As soon as he set foot on the ground, he drew a large key from his pocket. It creaked in the rusty lock, and when he opened the door the heavy smell of damp and mildew filled his nostrils. He hastened to push open the wooden shutters. The one huge room was exactly as it had been left last autumn, with its rough-hewn table, two long rickety benches, the old iron stove that drew so well propped up on a brick, and the bunks one above the other, as on board ship.

Nothing had changed. Yet it was almost as though Vincent had come up for the first time in his life. This year the hut would be his alone, and he saw it differently.

His first job was to light a fire to get rid of the damp and the cold. He kindled a whole basketful of dead wood. Then he set to and prepared his supper, heating water and peeling potatoes. Since he had made nearly the whole climb on Bichounette, he was not tired, but the tangy air of the heights had made him ravenously hungry. He sat down at one end of the table, which suddenly seemed vast and gave him a queer feeling in the pit of his stomach. He ate very quickly and soon had enough, which happens when you eat alone.

Afterwards, he went out. Bichounette, who was not tethered, was grazing peacefully, enjoying once more the taste of the mountain grasses, so different from those in the valley. The air had grown colder. It was evening now, one of those wonderful evenings that can only be found in the mountains. He walked over Wolf Ridge to look down on the valley. The lamps in the village, already lit, scarcely pierced the veil of blue haze thrown up by the torrent of the river. He looked for his own house, set back from the Servette on the outskirts of the village. He could picture his family gathered around the table with its steaming soup tureen, and a little shiver went through him. But he didn't for one moment regret leaving them—of course he didn't. He'd wanted to be all on his own like this, standing on his own feet like a man.

His eyes wandered over the mountain peaks, as they had done earlier when he had stopped on the way up. It was that sublime moment when the snow upon the mountains, pierced by the last arrows of the sun, glows with an incandescent light. It was as if the high peaks were stretching themselves to enjoy the warmth of the sun until the last possible moment. His eyes stayed longest on the most distant and highest peak of all.

"The Malacosta," he murmured. "The whole of that one is in Italy, I know."

Once more that unknown country came into his mind, and he imagined it perpetually bathed in the same rosy glow that just then enfolded the blazing mountains.

He knew quite well that the people living beyond the frontier were just like the French people of his own Lauzière, country folk who looked after their herds in the same sort of way, and who spoke French as easily as Italian. Never mind. It was another country, filled with the mystery of the unknown. He lowered his gaze from the Malacosta to Young Deer Pass. In the glow of the setting sun it seemed so near it was as though he could touch it with his finger. He found himself remembering the tales of bandits and smugglers that were often told around the fireside in the long winter evenings, in the valley. They were said to be true tales, of things that had happened in the last century, not so very long ago.

He could not help shuddering; but he was determined not to feel scared. After all, what could possibly happen to him?

He watched until the last afterglow of the setting sun had faded from the sky, then bedded Bichounette down for the night in the little lean-to adjoining the hut. It was dark when he went back inside. He lit the old kerosene lamp hanging on a wire pulley from a beam across the ceiling. The smoky flame was so dim that huge shadows filled the corners of the hut. He took two blankets from the deal chest, and spread them over the straw mattress on one of the bunks, but he did not feel ready for sleep. His solitude weighed upon him. He got up and took from his bag one of the books he had brought with him. He went to sit on a bench beneath the lamp, but he could not read either. There was too great a silence everywhere; he had never before realized how heavily silence weighs upon one who is alone.

He went out again into the icy air of a night sprinkled thickly with stars, and entered the little lean-to. On tiptoe he sought out Bichounette, who was on her side in the hay, her

legs stretched out. She snorted with pleasure as he settled down beside her and curled up in the hollow of her stomach against the pleasant warmth of her soft and silky coat. Bichounette was only an animal, but lying beside her, Vincent felt relaxed all over, and happy and peaceful again.

Then suddenly he was aware once more of the stillness around the hut, lost on the mountain like a ship on the ocean. He was filled with an ominous sense of foreboding—as if something terrible were about to happen. Although he told himself that he was being silly, his heart began pounding, and he found it extremely difficult to get to sleep.

2

A Shadow
in the Storm

IN the bright, warm sunlight of the next few days, Vincent worked hard at his mowing. For a change of pace he piled dead wood on the slope of Wolf Ridge, about twenty minutes' walk away from the hut. And he laughed to himself whenever he remembered his nervous fear that first night on the mountain.

But the lighthearted days on Wolf Ridge came to an abrupt end.

When Vincent opened his eyes on this particular morning, he thought he'd mistaken the time. On other days, the rising sun was filtering through the cracks of the shutters when he awoke, tracing long shafts of light on the floor. Today, although Vincent was sure that he had slept as long as he usually did, it was still quite dark. He sat bolt upright on his mattress as he heard a prolonged wailing, like strange music played by a thousand instruments, coming from the roof.

"The wind, it's the wind!"

He got up in the half-light, went to the window, pushed the shutters open, and received an icy slap full in the face.

"It's snow! Snow, in May!"

He quickly closed the window and stood in front of it. Huge snowflakes, hurled by the gusts of wind, came thick and fast to flatten themselves against the window-pane and vanish immediately. Outside, they did not melt; the grass, already flattened by the storm, was fast disappearing under a layer of white.

"Snow, in the middle of May! I don't suppose it will really settle, though."

There was nothing very extraordinary about it. There were years when snow had fallen later still, in June, and once even on July the third. This was a real snowstorm, however, like the ones that swept down in the winter and buried the villages beneath three feet of white foam in a single night.

"Work's off for today," Vincent said to himself. "And maybe tomorrow as well, if the sun doesn't break through quickly."

He lit the stove, which, spurred on by the wind, roared like a demon. He put some coffee on to heat, and cut himself three generous slices of bread. Then he opened the window to get the butter, which he always left on the window-sill outside in the fresh air. It was hard as a stone, just as it was in winter when everything froze.

"That's a bad sign," he thought.

When he had finished breakfast, he went to visit Bichounette, and was nearly bowled over on the threshold by a sudden gust of wind. The mule was upright in the lean-to, her long ears twitching all the time as they caught the queer noises, like the mournful howling of wolves, that were coming from the roof.

"It's all right, Bichounette," he said. "It's only a snowstorm. It won't last long."

He stroked the gentle animal and she lay down again, reassured by the presence of her master. Vincent stayed with her for a long time before he went back to the hut to get warm again.

The storm, far from blowing over, grew steadily worse, and the huge moist snowflakes of the early morning gave way to the fine dry crisp snow of winter.

"I'd be sorry for anyone caught just now in Young Deer Pass," Vincent said to himself. "It must be snowing even harder up there."

Since there was nothing else to do, he set to work conscientiously, hammered and sharpened all his scythes and mended the table leg that was loose. Then he picked up a book and settled on the floor in front of the stove. From time to time he looked out of the window, hoping to see some sign that the leaden sky would soon clear. But the heavy gray clouds were always there, and the snow came down relentlessly.

"The wind's not changed." He felt a bit anxious. "It's going to snow all day."

And so it did. The storm was still raging that evening, as though avenging the long spell of good weather that had brought the mountain early to flower.

Vincent, just as tired by a day of doing odds-and-ends as he would have been by a day's mowing, went to bed earlier than usual. His stock of wood was running low, and he would be saving fuel.

Snow was still falling when he opened the shutters the following morning, and outside the hut it reached almost to his knees. He had run out of wood, and he was growing really worried.

"It's my own fault. I should have brought a heap of wood back from the Ridge the other evening, instead of that load of fodder."

He burned bits of old planking that he found in the hut to keep the fire going, but the stove was as voracious as a flock of crows starved by the frost. At noon there was hardly enough heat to cook his midday meal.

"Nothing can be done about it. I'll just have to wait a bit."

The cold, however, gradually crept into the hut.

In the late afternoon the snow fell less thickly. When Vincent went out to look at the sky, the clouds did not seem quite so heavy, and the wind had died down. He decided to bring in a load of wood without more delay. He went into the lean-to and threw two big potbellied baskets across Bichounette's back.

The slope of Wolf Ridge where he had piled the wood was just above the famous Black Abyss. It was said in Lauzière that bears that felt the approach of death used to come and throw themselves into the abyss. Vincent knew that the snow would make his expedition a dangerous one, but he had no choice. The snow would not melt for two or three days, and he could not do without a fire for that length of time.

Fortunately Bichounette, being mountain bred, knew all the dangers and all the traps. She went forward slowly in the powdery white snow, feeling for the stony path with her hoofs. Only the snowflakes, settling in her long hairy ears, worried her.

Vincent kept looking anxiously at the clouds. The wind had suddenly started up again, and he wondered whether he should go on. He might as well, he had nearly reached the place.

Taking even more care, since he guessed that the precipice must be just below him, he came to the outskirts of the forest, where he found the woodpile covered with a thick blanket of snow. He set to work to fill the baskets as quickly as he could. But the sky darkened again rapidly and the snow fell thicker. At last Vincent finished loading, and tightened the mule's saddle girth with icy fingers.

"Come on, Bichounette! Let's get back quickly!"

It was just then that he saw a shadowy form at the edge of the forest, about fifty feet away. For one moment he wondered whether his eyes, blinded by the snow, were deceiving him. Could there be a man on this deserted mountainside? At the height of a storm? He must have lost his way, and he was in great danger of rolling down the steep slope and being swept along toward the Black Abyss.

"Don't move, Bichounette; wait there!"

The sudden thought that this man was in great danger had made him forget his own fear. He plunged through the curtain of snow in the direction in which the shadow had disappeared. All at once he saw it again, bent beneath the weight of a knapsack that seemed extraordinarily heavy. Making a megaphone of his hands, he shouted:

"Hola! Hola!"

The shadow, startled, came to an abrupt halt, turned around, and then moved off again into the squall, as if it had heard nothing. Vincent stood stock still. Didn't the man understand that he had called out simply to help him? The young mountain boy, deeply worried, set out after him in the snow that was still falling steadily. Then, just as Vincent was about to catch up with him, the man swung around and shook his fist threateningly. Vincent came to a halt, stunned, not

understanding; and as he stood there motionless,
yet ready in spite of all to go forward, the man
bent down, hurriedly molded some snow, and
threw a volley of hard icy snowballs at the boy.

More alarmed by the man's extraordinary atti-
tude than by his snowballs, Vincent drew back.
The stranger stared at him for a while; his fists
were clenched, and there was something menac-
ing about his thickset body outlined against the
sky. Then he disappeared once more into the icy
grayness, bent double beneath the weight of his
knapsack.

"I don't understand," Vincent kept saying to himself, trembling with shock. "I just don't understand."

He stood there in the snow, listening, wondering whether he ought to try once more to overtake the man. But the snow was coming down still more heavily, and he was in danger of losing his own way. So he went back to Bichounette, who was placidly waiting, her legs stiffened by the cold.

"Quick, let's go!"

The weather was growing steadily worse. It was impossible to see more than a few feet ahead, and Bichounette had difficulty in finding her former footholds. At last the hut loomed before them, a black blot on the leaden sky. Vincent swiftly unloaded the mule and settled her in the lean-to. Then he brought the wood in, and spread it all over the floor to dry quicker.

Out of breath because of the wind, which cut like a knife, and his long tramp through the snow, he was still shivering as he tried to relight his fire with great handfuls of dried hay.

He kept on saying to himself, "Why did that man go off like that? Where did he come from? Where's he going?"

He went on thinking about the strange meeting all the evening, and soon reached a point where he felt he should have tried much harder to help. Three times running he went out to the threshold of the hut, to listen, and to peer into the impenetrable darkness. He remembered all the stories he had heard in the long winter evenings in the valley, the terrifying stories of travelers lost in the storm who went mad with terror in the snow. Had that man gone out of his mind?

Vincent could not sleep that night. He got up several times, sure that he had heard cries for help: but each time it was only the wind wailing through the roof. And in spite of all he could do to prevent it, fear crowded in upon him, a hollow fear in no way due to any feeling of danger for himself. It was just fear—the sort that leaves you feeling terribly alone. He went out to Bichounette, as he had done that first night, and the mule seemed to be expecting him. He could not get the man's face out of his mind. He had not seen his features clearly: but the fleeting image he now called to mind was that of his harsh and furious expression.

When Vincent awoke the following morning, peace was restored to the mountains. The wind had suddenly dropped, and though the sky was still overcast, it was no longer snowing. He decided at once to go back to the wood to see whether he could find any traces of the stranger.

The snow, which must have fallen throughout most of the night, had leveled everything. He could see nothing that looked like a human shape on the slopes of the abyss, where it was not so deep. Nor did any voice reply to his calling.

"If anyone belonging to the region has disappeared, I shall find out when I go down to Lauzière," he said to himself. "If he's been killed on the rocks in the Black Abyss, he won't be found in any case until the snows melt."

The weather continued to clear up as the day went on. The tall peaks emerged from the clouds one by one, each as white as a sugar-loaf. A pale sun, shining like gold, appeared and began to melt the snow which streamed across the roof of the hut in long thin trickles of water.

Vincent was eager to take up his interrupted work again, but even though the snow was disappearing fast, the flattened grass would not be ready for scything for several days yet. It seemed a good idea to take advantage of this idle time to go down into the village and bring up fresh supplies. Vincent could not stop thinking about his strange encounter in the storm, and he wanted to know if anyone was missing from the valley.

When he arrived home at the farm, he said nothing about the matter. He was afraid that his father might jeer at him and say he had made it all up. His mother would think that he was afraid up there all alone and that it would be better if he did not go back to the hut. He went in search of Gilles, one of his closest friends. He told him what had happened on Wolf Ridge three days earlier. Gilles had not heard any talk. Together they looked through the papers: there was no reference to any disappearance.

"Perhaps you were mistaken," Gilles said. "You mistook a chamois seeking shelter for a man."

"No, Gilles, I know what I saw."

Could it be some stranger to the region, then, a man from the Piedmont district of Italy, who had come through Young Deer Pass? But why had he made off like that? Had he gone out of his mind in the storm, or was he in hiding because he had an uneasy conscience?

When Vincent went up to Wolf Ridge again, the mystery was still unsolved.

3

The
Midnight Visitor

IN the mountains even the most violent storms do not last very long once summer has come. A few hours are enough to wipe out all trace of them. Vincent came back to find the hut flooded with dazzling light and warmth, and the grass springing up already, greener than ever.

He set to work again resolutely, but he was still haunted by the thought of the man he had glimpsed in the blizzard. Once his work was finished for the day he went back several times to the place which overlooked the Black Abyss from a height of over nine hundred feet. The snow had completely disappeared, and he was able to venture down the steep slope as far as the tumbled mass of boulders that edged the precipice.

"No," he said to himself. "If a body were lying among those rocks, ravens would be circling above. The man I saw didn't fall in the snow; he found his way again."

After a while he almost forgot the encounter,

or rather tried to forget it; for sometimes of an evening he still thought he heard distant cries for help. So it was that one night he sat up in his bunk, his heart thudding, awakened by an unexpected noise. Was it another storm? Or was it Bichounette moving about on the other side of the partition?

He got up, listening hard. It was neither the wind nor Bichounette; the noise was coming from the door. It sounded as though someone were trying to open it, turning the latch and pushing against the boards with his shoulders to make it give way. Bracing himself against fear, Vincent stood still and silent, and waited. The noises stopped for a while, then started up again against the window shutters. After that there was another assault on the door. Could it be the man he had seen the other day? But why should he be prowling around the hut and trying to force an entry, after the way he had run off? Or was he a sneak thief? No—everyone in the region knew better than to leave anything of value in the summer huts.

Whoever he might be, Vincent got ready to defend himself against an attack, seizing hold of the sharpest sickle. Then, standing behind the door, he called out in a loud voice: "Who's there?"

Brandishing the sickle, he waited. The thudding on the door stopped at once, and he heard the sound of footsteps outside, fading rapidly away into the distance. He wrenched open the door. In the clear cold darkness lit by a shining crescent moon he could see a black shape outlined against the sky, about fifty feet from the hut. He knew at once that this was not the man he had seen before. This one was tall and slim, the other had been short and stocky. He shouted at the top of his voice:

"What do you want?"

The man did not answer, but neither did he run off.

"What do you want?" Vincent said again. The stranger moved a few steps toward him, and then stood still.

"I thought the hut was empty. I was hoping for a night's shelter."

Vincent knew at once that he was an Italian by his accent. The stories of smugglers and bandits came into his mind, but there was nothing to be scared of in that shaking, anxious voice. He went forward, and the stranger waited for him to come near. The mountain lad saw then that he was a young man, about twenty or twenty-five at most, bowed beneath the weight of an enormous rucksack.

"You're shivering with cold," said Vincent. "Come in and get warm."

The stranger hesitated, and then followed him. The flickering light of the kerosene lamp revealed an exhausted and troubled face. Vincent was still holding the sickle, and the man

said, "Don't be scared. I don't mean you any harm. And I've no weapons, except for this."

He drew a knife from his pocket and threw it on the table.

"Take it, you can give it back when I leave."

Vincent did not touch it, only put away the sickle. Heartened by this mark of confidence, the man gave a little smile, unstrapped his rucksack, and sank wearily down onto a bench, utterly exhausted.

"I got lost in the mountains. I walked for hours without being able to find my way again."

Vincent lit the stove, which soon began to roar, and the stranger stretched his hands toward it to enjoy its warmth. There was a long silence.

"Where do you come from?" Vincent asked. The stranger did not answer, and then Vincent saw tears trembling on his lashes. He had never before seen a man cry, and he supposed it must be because of exhaustion and cold and hunger.

"Would you like something to eat?"

The man shook his head. "I brought food with me. It's just that I'm absolutely all in. I'd no idea it was so far."

Silence fell once more in the hut; then the stranger, after a noticeable hesitation, said, "Is it far off—the valley the train goes through?"

"About three or four hours' walk, if you take the short cuts; but they're dangerous at night."

The man sighed and said no more. Vincent

was dying to ask some more questions, but his visitor looked too unhappy, and the boy noticed that he was still shivering.

"I'll heat up some coffee. That's what you need."

The man agreed, and swallowed the scalding drink almost in one gulp.

"If you'd like to spend the night here," Vincent offered, "there are plenty of mattresses."

The stranger looked at the bunk indicated by Vincent, then turned to him.

"No, I won't do that. You'd be scared. You'd stay awake all night. Your fire has warmed me through. Now I'll go and find shelter where I won't be putting anyone out."

"There are no other huts on Wolf Ridge. And believe me, I'm not afraid."

The stranger was persuaded to stay. Vincent prepared a bunk by spreading blankets over it; then, when the man was settled, he put out the lamp, and went back to bed. He found it impossible to sleep, though it was not fear that kept him awake. It was more the intense curiosity mixed with anxiety that he felt about the fate of this man, who was clearly unhappy.

An hour went by, and still Vincent could not sleep—nor could the stranger. Vincent heard him sigh and turn restlessly on the mattress stuffed with maize leaves.

"Perhaps he's ill," he thought.

He got out of bed and touched the man on

the shoulder, making him jump.

"Do you feel all right?" he asked.

The stranger did not answer, but suddenly took hold of Vincent's hand.

"You're wondering where I've come from . . . where I'm going to, aren't you?"

He too got out of bed. Vincent relit the lamp and they sat down at the table, facing each other. The man sighed.

"You can take my word for it, I'm not a thief nor a bandit. My name is Alberto Conti. I'm Italian, and I come from the village of Argentera, the other side of the pass. My family lives there. I had to leave home."

The man lowered his head as though he were ashamed of what he had just said. He drew a shabby wallet from the pocket of his jacket, took small photographs from it and handed them to Vincent. One was of a woman with classic features, no longer young; the other of a girl, not much more than a child, with a sensitive face and expressive eyes.

"My mother," he explained. "And my little sister Rosalba. The three of us lived together, and we were happy . . . then there was a burglary in the village and I was accused. But I swear by Our Lady that I did not do it."

He crossed himself to show that he was speaking the truth. Then he added, "The police came to my home several times. It was clear that they were going to arrest me, so I thought it better to leave my mother and sister and take refuge in France. I know some Piedmontese who will take me in. I shall try to find work, and then I could perhaps send some money to my mother and sister."

While he was speaking, Vincent had kept the two small photographs in his hand, looking first at one, then at the other.

"Yes," the man murmured under his breath. "It's hard to leave the people you love. My father died ten years ago. I had a brother, older than me, but he was killed in an accident in Milan. There's only my little sister Rosalba now; she's thirteen. She cried herself sick when I left."

"Rosalba," Vincent said her name, looking at the small face and dark eyes of the photograph.

"She is very fond of me. She refused to believe that I'd done anything wrong, even when appearances were against me. She'll be crying now, wondering where I am and whether I've lost my way in the mountains."

Slowly the man took the photographs back, looked lovingly at them, and then replaced them in his wallet. It was clear that he was relieved to have spoken out, and that he was happier now he had been able to talk about his family.

"I'm so sorry," he said, noting that Vincent could scarcely keep his eyes open. "I'm keeping you up. Go back to bed. I think I'll be able to sleep now too."

Vincent put out the lamp, and they both went

back to their bunks. His mind at rest, the man wrapped himself up in his blankets, and soon his regular breathing showed that he was asleep.

"How unhappy he is," thought Vincent. "I could tell at once by his eyes that he wasn't telling lies. I'm absolutely certain that he's done nothing wrong."

Before he could stop himself he had thought of that other man who had fled before him in the snow. Was there any link between these two strangers?

"Tomorrow," he told himself, "as soon as he wakes up, I'll tell him what I saw the other night in the storm."

At last he fell asleep, utterly exhausted and worn out by excitement.

When Vincent opened his eyes again after a heavy sleep thronged with strange dreams, the sun was creeping into the hut through the chinks in the shutters. Sitting up in his bunk, his first thought was to see whether the man was still asleep. The bunk was empty. Quickly he got up and crossed the threshold into Bichounette's stable in the lean-to. Nothing. The man had disappeared. Climbing along Wolf Ridge, Vincent called in all directions. No reply. So he went back to the hut, and pushed open the shutters. And then, as he turned, he caught sight of something shining on the table. It was a watch, an old-fashioned silver watch with an engraved case. And this watch was serving as a paperweight to a note on which he read the words: "To thank you."

Vincent was deeply touched. This watch was probably the most precious thing the Italian possessed, after the photographs of his mother and sister. He had given it up so that Vincent would know how glad he had been to meet someone who shared his misery and believed that he spoke the truth.

"Yes," Vincent said to himself, turning the watch over in his fingers, "I'm quite sure he was as honest as the day. But I can't accept such a present, I have no right to. I only did what anyone would have done."

He looked again at the watch, which was still going, and placed it carefully on the beam above the stove.

4

Young Deer Pass

WITH the return of the good weather, it became possible to make up for lost time. Bichounette made several journeys every day, bringing back huge baskets filled with sweet-smelling hay. Vincent, making full use of his strength and his freedom, came back each night exhausted; yet this healthy tiredness did not bring sleep in its train. He was hoping that Alberto would come back and knock on the door of the hut. He kept seeing the young man's sad face and remembering how he had wept like a child before him. Why had he been accused if he were not guilty? Were people so unjust, then? He also kept seeing the photographs that had meant so much to the stranger, and above all the face of the little Italian girl. He tried to picture her at home over there, on the other side of the frontier. She would probably be crying, no longer daring to go out, imagining that everyone was pointing at her. Could no one do anything, then, for her and her mother? He was filled with a furious anger against those who had accused her brother.

One evening at the beginning of June, when his day's work was finished, Vincent sat looking at the mountains glowing with gold, and fixed his eyes for a long time on Young Deer Pass. It had never seemed so near as it did then, in the clear air freed now from the mists of the day.

"I'll go across the frontier tomorrow," he said to himself. "I'll go and see Rosalba, and give back her brother's watch."

Mountain bred, he knew that the way to the pass, nearly eight thousand feet up, would be long and difficult; but he would not go alone. Bichounette was both surefooted and tireless.

As soon as the after-glow had faded from the peaks, he went back to the hut. His father had at some time pinned an old map of the region on the door of the hut. Vincent examined this now by the light of the kerosene lamp, which he had unhooked from the ceiling. The map was yellowed by the smoke from the stove, and its folds were worn. Time, light and soot had destroyed its colors, but even so Vincent was able to trace with his forefinger the erratic line of little black crosses placed end to end that marked the frontier.

He had greater difficulty in finding Young Deer Pass, a microscopic zigzag line of dots that showed the muletrack. Finally, on the other side of the mountain range, he saw the name

Argentera, not so faded as the names of French villages that had often been pointed out. He tried to work out the distance, as a mountaineer always does, in hours of walking. It might take five or six, although it would be an hour or two shorter with Bichounette.

He decided to set out the following morning, and went to bed early so as to be fit for the journey. Yet he found it impossible to get to sleep. He had a strong feeling that he was on the brink of an extraordinary adventure, filled with events as yet unknown, in which he must inevitably become involved.

When he got up, it was so early that the sun had not yet climbed the barrier of the peaks. It might not even appear at all, for the sky had clouded over during the night.

"I might have known," Vincent said to himself, "for it's always a sign of bad weather when the mountains look too near in the evening."

It did not worry him: on the contrary, he would rather have this overcast weather than the mountain sun burning like fire, parching his mouth and scorching Bichounette's back.

He followed the line of Wolf Ridge, crossed a small wood, went along a mountain meadow, and rejoined the path, which twisted and turned as it climbed above the last grasslands. Soon the grass grew scarce, and was replaced by masses of fallen rock, where even Bichounette would have lost her footing, had she made one false

step. As they climbed higher, and the clouds came lower, skimming the crests one by one, the air grew sharper.

"Come on, Bichounette, go a bit faster!"

The gallant mule was climbing steadily, straight-legged. From time to time Vincent dismounted and walked behind to rest her, hanging on to her tail, as mountain folk often do. Soon they came to the cloud ceiling, the treacherous mist that conceals precipices, and soaks you to the skin. Bichounette brought her long hairy ears forward now, for the echo of her hoofs tapping on the rock would serve her better than her eyes.

For two solid hours they went forward in the mist. Vincent was beginning to wonder whether they had not gone astray when suddenly Bichounette came to a halt, her forelegs braced, her hindlegs bent, as though she had just caught sight of an abyss. Vincent quickly jumped down. There was only empty space ahead; yet they had not come to a ravine, for the path went on, plunging rapidly down into the drowned depths of the swirling mist.

"Don't move, Bichounette!"

Vincent walked on a few steps and found a wooden post, all but knocked over by the wind. Once it had been painted, but frost and snow and the sun had eaten away the color. However, he could still see traces of green, white and red on one side, and on the other red, white and a little blue.

"It's the frontier! I've reached the frontier!" His heart began to beat faster, and he shook with excitement. The frontier! Maybe shadowy customs officers or policemen would loom now out of the mist! He knew quite well, of course, that no one guarded Young Deer Pass. It was too difficult, too often snowed up, and it no longer echoed to the tramping of smugglers' boots.

It was extremely cold, and the wind promised snow any time now. Fear of the unknown, of the mysterious country that lay beyond the post, held Vincent back for a moment at the head of the pass; but a greater force made him go on.

"Get going, Bichounette!"

The mule too drew back a moment before this emptiness, but her master had spoken, and so she obeyed. With infinite care she set out down the slope, so very much steeper than on the French side. They both had the impression of descending into a bottomless pit; but soon they had burst through the cloud ceiling, and a valley appeared, less green and more rugged perhaps than that of Lauzière, but very like it.

"So this is Italy." Vincent was astonished that the place was not more different.

He stopped to look at the old map, which he had brought with him, for he could see no sign of a village. Argentera must be hidden behind a fold of the mountain that reared its great crest over there on the left. For an hour the steep descent continued, jarring the legs of the mule, strong though they were. At last, Argentera suddenly appeared before them, backed against the mountain, and facing south. Vincent's heart quickened again. Wolf Ridge seemed very far away, but he did not regret his journey.

The air grew gradually softer, the countryside less wild and more distinct. The village, playing hide-and-seek with him according to the twists and turns of the path, grew larger each time it reappeared.

He came at last to a house, the first he had seen in the four hours of his journey. Its roof was covered with tiles, not with shingles as in Lauzière. It was a wretched sort of place, but he decided nevertheless to stop and ask the way to Rosalba's house. He jumped off the mule and knocked at the door. A woman came out, looking with a mixture of curiosity and distrust at this boy who was a stranger to the valley.

"Is that Argentera on the other side of the torrent?"

As soon as she heard Vincent's accent, the woman knew that he came from the other side of the frontier.

"Yes, it's Argentera," she said in a disagreeable voice. "There's no other village along this valley."

Her French was correct, but her accent was so peculiar that Vincent could hardly understand what she said.

"I'm looking for Rosalba Conti's house."

The woman's eyes widened with astonishment. "Rosalba? . . . What do you want with her?"

"I want to see her, to speak to her."

He had no time to say more. Another face had appeared in the doorway, that of an unshaven man wearing a thick checkered jacket with large buttons. He had a bandage around his head, and his right arm was in a sling. Vincent instinctively drew back.

"Don't be scared, my boy—I was cutting wood in the mountain when I fell and got hurt. Now if I heard aright you've come through Young Deer Pass, and you want to see Rosalba Conti?" Lowering his voice he added, "You know what has happened?"

"I've heard. Where does she live?"

"We'll tell you, but just come in for a moment to warm up—you're soaked to the skin from the mountain mist."

The man's hand propelled him into the house, and Vincent dared not resist. The woman, for her part, now abandoned the surly manner in which she had spoken to him before.

"Sit down. I'm sure you could do with a glass of something after that long trek through the mountains."

Very reluctantly, he sat down on the stool that was pushed toward him. He was embarrassed by this suddenly eager welcome, since he did not like the man or the woman very much. He wondered whether all the people in the region were like these two. The woman took a bottle from a cupboard, and filled two small glasses. The cider tasted very much like that made in Lauzière.

"So you've come from over yonder especially to see Rosalba," said the man with the bandaged head. "Didn't you know that her brother stole the gold cross of Santa Anna, and then ran off before they could arrest him? Of course, at first no one believed he had done it—a crime like that, stealing a cross from a church. But there it is, you can't go against the facts. He must be the one . . . and the proof is that he's cleared out. Poor Alberto!"

"Alberto is not a thief," Vincent replied. "I'm quite certain about that."

The man looked curiously at him, then

nodded his head.

"You've seen him then? Spoken to him?"

"He spent the night in my hut, when he escaped to France to go into hiding. He swore that he'd done nothing wrong, and I know he spoke the truth. When he went, he left his silver watch behind to thank me. And I've come to give that watch back where it belongs."

He drew it from his pocket, and the man and the woman looked closely at it.

"So you say that he spent a night under your roof when he set out for France."

"In the summer hut. I've been cutting hay for the last three weeks."

"Near Young Deer Pass?"

"On Wolf Ridge, above the village of Lauzière, not very far from the Black Abyss."

"Black Abyss," the man repeated. "Oh yes, we've heard of it even on this side of the frontier. They say it's very deep." Then, gruffly, as though he wanted to change the subject, he said, "So you came all this way to bring the watch back, the watch of a thief found guilty by the whole village."

"Where is his house?" Vincent got up, ready to go, regretting that he had said so much to these strangers.

As they all three stood on the threshold, the woman pointed out a house on the other side of the torrent, a house with freshly painted red shutters.

Vincent mounted Bichounette, who had been

peacefully waiting for him in front of the door, and went down the path without looking back, aware that behind him both the man and the woman were watching. Just as he came to the wooden bridge flung across the torrent, he drew back. What he had just heard made him stop and think for a moment. Suppose Alberto were guilty? Suppose Rosalba and her mother were his accomplices? In spite of these new doubts, a voice within him insisted that his first impression of Alberto had been the right one.

So, pressing his heels into Bichounette's sides, he set off for the bridge, and crossed the torrent.

5

Rosalba's Story

WITH its freshly painted shutters, and the geraniums just coming into bloom in the tiny flowerbeds each side of the door, Rosalba's house seemed to offer an immediate welcome when Vincent came to a halt in front of it. But why were the shutters half closed? It was not yet siesta time.

He dismounted and knocked. No one answered. He knocked again, a little louder, but with no result. Yet he thought he heard quiet footsteps within the house. A boy came by, and Vincent asked him whether Rosalba was at home.

Instead of replying, the boy ran off as if the devil were on his heels and shouted from a distance, "The house of the *ladro*! The house of the *ladro*!"

Vincent knew that *ladro* is the Italian for thief. The word shocked him. Then it was true, as the man had said, that the whole village was against

Alberto. He took a few steps backward, so that he could look over the house from top to bottom, then went forward again and, without knocking, stood close to the door and called, "Please open. I've got news of Alberto."

There was another long silence; then at last the door opened just a crack. A face appeared, a little panic-stricken face that Vincent recognized at once. When she saw a stranger standing there, the girl drew back and closed the door.

Vincent spoke again: "Do open the door, Rosalba. You don't know me, but I know you. Alberto sent me to you."

The door was half opened again.

"Who are you then?" an anxious voice demanded.

"Your brother's friend. He gave me this, and I'm bringing it back to you."

He drew the watch out of his pocket; the sight of it brought a cry of surprise from the Italian girl.

"Oh! His watch! You really have seen him, then?" She took the watch and turned it over in her hands as though to make sure that it was the right one. Then she said, with her finger at her lips, "Come in quietly. Mother's ill and she's asleep just now."

He tethered the mule at the side of the house, so that she could not trample the geraniums by the door, and went into the kitchen which he found in semi-darkness. As he turned instinctively to the window, where a slender ray of sunlight was filtering through, the girl said angrily:

"We daren't open the shutters anymore. It's because of the village boys. They're behaving badly toward us. They often throw stones as they go past the house."

She switched on the light, and they stood face to face. Once again Rosalba's dark eyes showed their anxiety.

"What's your name? How did you get to know my brother? Where is he? . . . Has anything happened to him?"

"I'm Vincent Missillier. I'm staying in our summer hut on the other side of Young Deer Pass. That's where I saw your brother."

He told her how, one night, Alberto, believing the hut to be empty, had tried to break in to get some rest.

"I knew at once that he was not guilty—he looked so desperately unhappy when he showed me your photograph and your mother's."

"We've had no news of him since he left Argentera for France. Where is he now? Is he staying with you?"

"When I woke up the next morning, he'd already gone. Before he left, he put his watch on the table for me . . . as a present, to thank me . . . but I can't keep it, and so I've brought it back to you."

"Oh, is that why you came?"

"Yes, and also . . ."

He hesitated a moment, because he was embarrassed.

"And also because I wanted to let you know that he'd come to no harm crossing the mountains . . . and to tell you I'm quite sure that one day the real thief will be found, since Alberto has done nothing wrong."

"Oh, you too, you believe . . ." There were tears of joy in Rosalba's eyes.

Just then they heard a noise above their heads, and a voice asked, "Who's there? I told you not to let anyone in!"

Rosalba dried her tears quickly, and mounted the wooden stairs. Vincent could hear her speaking quietly to her mother; then she reappeared.

"Mother would like to see you."

Vincent mounted the narrow stairway and found himself in a small attic room, scrupulously clean and with a certain charm. Lying in the middle of a wooden bed was a woman with a sad face and graying hair.

"Oh!" she said, sitting up against her pillows, "Rosalba has just told me you've seen Alberto . . . he's safe and in France . . . and you've come all that way across the mountains to let us know."

She stretched out both arms to Vincent, who went over to her bedside and told her everything he had just told Rosalba. When he finished, she sighed and said:

"We were so happy, the three of us, in this little house . . . and now the whole village is against us. Yet, if you only knew my son. . . . There's not another man in the whole of Piedmont who works as hard as he does. He had no reason to steal the cross. We're not rich, but he was earning his living all right as a mason, and we didn't ask more than that. As you can see, grief has made me ill. . . . If the real culprit isn't found, I will die of shame!"

She squeezed Vincent's hands again, then grew concerned about him.

"You must be worn out, and very hungry after such a long journey. Look after him, Rosalba."

Vincent assured her that he was neither tired nor hungry. He had brought food with him, and he intended to go back through the pass before dusk. He would, however, stay an hour longer, so as to rest Bichounette.

He went down to the kitchen again with Rosalba.

"Do you like *polenta*?" she asked him.

"I've never had it."

"It's a sort of cake we make in Piedmont with maize flour. I think you'd like it."

He watched her busy about the kitchen. She was quick and graceful in her movements, and she made him feel like a big brother anxious to look after her. He realized all at once that he had not made this long journey simply to bring the watch back, but also to help Alberto.

"Rosalba," he said, "all I know is that a gold cross was stolen from a chapel. That's all. I wish you would tell me . . ."

"Didn't Alberto tell you all about it?"

"I didn't like to ask him. He seemed much too unhappy."

The girl lifted wide astonished eyes to his.

"Then how could you know he wasn't guilty?"

"I don't know, Rosalba, I just felt that he wasn't."

She hung her head and murmured in a sad voice, "I'm afraid that you'll be against my brother, like the rest of the village, if I tell you."

"I don't think I will, Rosalba. I wish you'd tell me."

There was a long silence, then Rosalba got up

and drew Vincent to the window. She pointed toward the mountains.

"Do you see that white patch up there, over-looking the village? That's the chapel of Santa Anna. As far back as anyone can remember, she has protected travelers crossing the mountains. You reach the chapel along a path that ends in steps cut out of the rock. There was a cross in that chapel, a huge gold cross fixed to the end wall behind the wooden statue of Santa Anna."

For a long time Vincent stared at the little square of white stone standing out against its rocky background.

"Was the cross kept safe behind locked doors?" he asked.

"The mountain chapels in our region have no doors, so that any passer-by can come in to pray."

"A gold cross in a chapel open to anyone who happens by! Surely some sneak thief or other must have been tempted?"

Rosalba's head drooped again.

"That's just the point, Vincent. Apart from the parish priest—we call him the *padre*—no one knew that the cross was real gold. It was given to the village about three hundred years ago by the Duke of Mantua as an offering of thanks to Providence for saving him from an attack by bears while he was training in the mountains. It was placed in the chapel of Santa Anna, as the Duke requested. But so that it would not be stolen, it was painted to look like wood, like the statue in front of it. Only the *padres* of the parish knew the secret.

"This spring a huge avalanche came down the mountainside when the snows melted. Boulders fell on the chapel, and it had to be repaired. One day the *padre* came to see my brother; for Alberto is the best stonemason in the valley, and the *padre* trusted him. The cross had come loose, and would have to be taken down. As it was extraordinarily heavy, and the paint had peeled off here and there, my brother found out that it was made of gold. He told the *padre*, who of course already knew, and he made my brother swear to keep the secret. He did not even tell my mother, or me. We knew only the day after it was stolen."

Vincent sighed, as unhappy as Rosalba. "When did the cross disappear?"

"Three weeks ago. The *padre* himself saw one morning that it was gone. It had been loosened and torn from the wall, in spite of the fact that my brother had fixed it securely."

"Perhaps someone besides the *padre* and your brother knew that it was made of gold?"

Rosalba hung her head again.

"Perhaps . . . yes, of course . . . but there's another thing. It snowed a little the night of the theft, and in the morning they found footprints around the chapel. They were my brother's."

"All prints of heavy mountain boots look alike, Rosalba."

She shook her head.

"No, not all. When my brother was only a boy he had a fall on the mountains, and his right foot was a bit deformed as a result of it. He has to have his boots specially made by the shoemaker at Sallega—that's a village down the valley. His right boot is a little wider than the left."

There was another pause.

"And that's not all," added the girl. "They found something else near the chapel—a tilelayer's hammer belonging to my brother. As you can see, everything points to him. And now that I've told you everything, I'm sure that you too . . ."

Vincent did not answer. It was true that everything pointed to Alberto, and just for the moment he was shaken. Then he pulled himself together, took Rosalba's hands and squeezed them gently.

"No, I don't believe it. Your brother isn't guilty. If he had set out to steal the gold cross of Santa Anna, he would not have chosen a night when it was snowing, nor would he have left his special hammer behind. What did he say in his own defense?"

"What you have just said, Vincent . . . but no one believed him."

Vincent turned it all over in his mind for a long time.

"I don't understand any of it," he said. "But I'm quite certain that one day the real thief will be found."

They were still standing by the window. As Vincent looked up again at the chapel he noticed all at once that the weather had clouded over. The hour he had allowed himself had long since gone.

"I must go, Rosalba; it's more than time."

"Already!"

There was such deep regret in that "Already!" that he was very much moved.

"I must, Rosalba. But I promise you I'll come back. I promise I'll help you. I'm sure your brother will soon return."

The little girl did not answer, but a faint smile appeared around her mouth. Vincent's words had cheered her.

He went to untie Bichounette, and was just going to mount her when Rosalba came toward him.

"Here," she said, "take this with you!" She held out to him a little statuette of painted wood.

"It's a little Santa Anna," she said, "like the one up there; every house in Argentera has one. Take her. She will look after you in the mountains."

He accepted the little statue, and slipped it carefully into his pocket, then for the last time took Rosalba's hand.

"We'll put things right for your brother, Rosalba."

He set off quickly, without a backward look

at the little house with the red shutters. It was late, and he had to get through the pass before nightfall. He could not, however, refrain from looking up at the white chapel, and suddenly he wanted to visit it before setting out on the road to the pass. Turning left, he took the rocky path that climbed above the village and led to the foot of the great rock on which the chapel stood. The path ended in steps cut into the rock itself, just as Rosalba had described it. He jumped off Bichounette and mounted them on foot.

The chapel was quite small and had a gray slate roof. Inside, the painted wooden statue of Santa Anna was almost drowned in a sea of mountain flowers brought by pious hands . . . those of Rosalba among them, perhaps. There was a great hole in the end wall where the gold cross should have been. The thief had certainly been put to a great deal of trouble in getting it down. Vincent walked around the chapel several times, looking for a clue. But what? The police and the *padre* had been there several times already. There could be nothing left to find.

"Alberto is not guilty," he thought. "The real thief is someone who also knew that the cross was made of gold, but without anyone suspecting that he knew. He's the one who made people believe it was Rosalba's brother, to cover his own traces."

Heavy-hearted, Vincent walked slowly down

the stone steps. Just as he was approaching Bichounette, a voice called out to him from down the path.

"What are you doing here, when you ought to be hurrying off to get across the mountain? Can't you see that it's nearly dusk, and darkness will overtake you while you're still on your way?"

It was the man with the bandaged head and the arm in a sling, at whose house he had stopped to ask his way. Since Vincent did not hide his surprise at finding him there, the man added in the same breath, "I was busy cutting kindling wood in this thicket. I recognized your mule."

Then he came up to Vincent and said, "So you

saw Rosalba and her mother? Did they tell you all that's happened? I'm sorry for them. . . . There's so little anyone can do for them, especially now that Alberto has gone across the frontier."

Vincent did not answer. There was something false and unctuous in the man's voice that he did not like.

"In any case," said the Italian, "you'd be a fool to get yourself mixed up in this affair. Take my advice and don't ever come back to Argentera. You're French, and you might easily run into trouble with the Italian police. What's more, people in these parts don't much care for interference in their own concerns. . . . So goodbye, my boy; I wish you a safe journey . . . and remember what I've said."

Vincent mounted the mule without replying, and descended the path; but when, about three hundred feet lower down, he turned for a last look at Santa Anna, the man was still standing in the middle of the road, silhouetted against a background of bluish mountains. And suddenly Vincent felt his heart miss a beat, for that silhouette had brought another to mind. He could not understand why he had not been struck by the resemblance earlier in the day, unless it was because of the bandaged head and the arm in a sling. For now he was seeing again the shadow he had seen in the storm: the same broad shoulders, the same thick neck, and above all, the same short, bandy legs. When he had caught that fleeting glimpse of the man running away through the snow, he had noticed the bent legs, but he had thought them due to the weight of the knapsack.

There could be no doubt about it; the man at whose house he had stopped by chance was the man he had met near Wolf Ridge.

6

Footprints

VINCENT had come down into the valley for supplies. He wanted to get hold of Gilles as soon as possible, so early on that particular morning he knocked on his friend's door. They went and sat side by side on the parapet of the old La Servette Bridge: it was hardly ever used now that the new one had been built in the center of the little market town. No one would disturb them there, and the rushing torrent would muffle their conversation.

Vincent spoke of his expedition to Argentera, and said a great deal about Rosalba and Alberto, and the Italian with the strange appearance who was so like the man in the snowstorm.

"You see, Gilles, when Alberto was telling me about it the other day, I had a sort of premonition—I don't know why. It suddenly seemed as if that man running away from me in the storm must be linked somehow with the theft . . . and now, I'm absolutely certain that he is."

Gilles shook his head. He was the same age as

Vincent, but the two boys were not at all alike. Gilles was as stolid and level-headed as Vincent was easily roused to wild enthusiasm.

"What makes you so sure, Vincent?"

"That resemblance. It was the most striking thing!"

"Have you forgotten, Vincent, that two weeks ago, when I asked you what the man was like, you couldn't even tell me whether he was dark and had a moustache like so many Piedmontese."

"Perhaps so. . . . But I swear I'm not mistaken about that silhouette."

"Even if you're right about that, what's the connection with the stolen cross? We all know that smugglers still exist . . . and they don't like meeting anyone when they're on the job. Are you sure you aren't imagining things? Remember how we often laughed at you at school because you got all worked up about nothing?"

"If you'd seen that man as I saw him, you wouldn't say that. There was something shifty about him. And why was his wife so eager for me to come in as soon as I mentioned Rosalba, after she'd practically jumped down my throat? And why was the man hanging about the chapel when I was on my way home? He couldn't possibly have been cutting wood, as he said he was, with his arm in a sling. And why was he so insistent that I should not come back to Argentera? He all but threatened me!"

Gilles, a little smile on his lips, put a hand on his friend's shoulder.

"You believe, then, that this man is afraid of you for some reason or other. But surely a man who has done something wrong is only afraid of someone who can give him away . . . and you don't know anything, except what Rosalba has told you. For example, you couldn't even prove that he is the man you met on the mountain, since you yourself are the only witness."

Gilles's comment was fair enough. In effect, the man had nothing to fear. Vincent began to think it over.

"True enough," Vincent said. "I don't know for sure. But there's something else. You forget that the gold cross was stolen during the snowstorm, that it weighed a great deal, and that the man who ran off into the storm had a knapsack on his back that bent him nearly double."

"And that makes you believe the Italian carried off this precious cross to hide it here in France?"

"Probably. All the Italian newspapers must have been full of the theft. It would be difficult for the thief to get rid of the cross in his own country."

Vincent stroked his forehead.

"Anyway, one thing I'm pretty well sure of," he continued, "and that is that the thief is someone from Argentera, someone who knew Alberto very well."

"Why?"

"You may be sure that if Alberto were guilty, he would not have left his special hammer behind near the chapel. And he would have chosen a day when there was no snow, so as to leave no footprints, particularly since one of his feet is slightly deformed. It's perfectly clear to me that the thief covered his own tracks by taking very good care that suspicion should fall on Alberto."

Vincent seemed so sure of himself again, and his reasoning was so logical, that Gilles began to take him more seriously.

"Maybe you're right after all, Vincent. . . . But what do you mean to do then? Tell the police? Warn the French customs officers?"

"I did think I would. But if I tell them I saw a man running away during the storm, they'll think I imagined it. There's been no accident, nor has any disappearance been reported. And if I tell them about my expedition to Argentera, they'll just shrug their shoulders and say that what happens in Argentera is no concern of theirs. And they'll want to know if I had my papers to cross the frontier."

"It certainly is complicated. . . . And if the thief really did come into France to hide the gold cross, you may be sure that he's taken every precaution against its being found."

Vincent felt depressed. Alberto had come suddenly into his mind. He saw him again sitting beneath the lamp looking at the photographs. He saw Rosalba's delicate little face too, and her mother's sad one. He had promised to help the little Italian girl as he left the house with the red shutters; was there nothing to be done?

"Nothing," he murmured. "Nothing. No, that's just not possible."

There was another silence, until Gilles asked: "What do you mean to do then?"

"I don't know. And yet I must do something."

Gilles looked at his friend and took him by the hand.

"Listen, Vincent, I want to help you. You know I'm finished with school this week. I could join you up there, if you find you need me. My father would certainly let me come and stay for a few days. But how can you let me know whether you want me?"

Vincent thought it over.

"I could signal to you with my lantern. That's it. You come and stand on this bridge every evening about nine for at least a week. Look—you can see the hut quite well from here. If I swing the lantern like this, with my arm stretched out, then it means you must come up."

"Right, I'll be here every evening, Vincent."

The two friends shook hands to seal the agreement, then left the stone bridge and went their separate ways.

As on the other occasions, Vincent had to set out on his return journey early in the afternoon, so as to reach the hut before nightfall. He went back to the farm and began to pile together his supplies for the week, and the other things he needed to take back. His mother noticed his pre-occupied air, and the nervous movements he made.

"Vincent," she said, "I haven't said anything up till now, but each time you come back I sense a change in you. Is it the loneliness of the mountains that is getting you down?"

"Honestly, Mother, I like it up there tremendously. I've never known the days to go so fast."

"Then what is it, my dear Vincent?"

He wanted to tell her everything, but he was afraid that she would worry about him. He wondered if it was wrong to hide his anxieties from her: but he was doing a man's job; he had every right to spare those he loved from anxiety. Besides, he was in no danger up there. He just smiled gently.

"Nothing's the matter, Mother, honestly."

His mother sighed. She was just a little nervous for this tall son who was keeping his thoughts to himself.

"If you like, you can take Miski back with you," she offered. "He's not really needed here now that the cattle are on the high pastures. He'll be company for you and Bichounette."

Miski was a young Alsatian dog, about eighteen months old, in peak condition, so powerful that he could bowl a man over simply by standing and placing his forepaws on the man's shoulders. He was an intelligent animal trained to take the cows to pasture, and an excellent watchdog.

Vincent saw no point in it, since he most certainly was not afraid up there, but in the end he decided to take Miski, partly to set his mother's fears at rest, partly because, after all, a dog can be useful when you are on your own.

Two hours later, with Miski capering around the mule, Vincent set out again for the hut. His adventure had seemed far away and unreal to him throughout the day spent in the valley, but as he climbed it filled his mind again to the exclusion of everything else. He kept his eyes on Young Deer Pass, and everything seemed to grow clearer, as though his thinking were quickened by the purity of the air. His faith in Alberto, for a moment shaken by Gilles, stood firm again.

He reached Wolf Ridge just before nightfall, and once more he was enfolded by the great silence. He found the hut exactly as he had left it, its door and shutters closed. And then in front of the step he saw, in the earth softened by the previous day's shower, footprints that were certainly not his own. Someone had come to the hut in his absence. Miski, who seemed to be intrigued by an alien smell, roamed this way and that, his nose to the ground. It was clear that the stranger had gone around the hut, seeking a way in. Vincent hesitated to open the door for a moment, as though he expected to find someone inside. But Miski was with him and he wasn't afraid. He pushed open the door, looked all around in the half light, then swung back the shutters to let in the light. There was nothing out of place, no blanket unfolded on the bunks. The stranger had clearly not entered. Partially reassured, Vincent went out. Under the porch roof, he had left a sickle hanging beside a leather belt to which was fastened a cow's horn holding a grindstone. Suddenly it seemed to him that they were not quite in the same position.

He went up to them. Something wrapped in paper was slipped into the bottom of the horn. He drew out the little rolled packet, and a wad of banknotes escaped from it, Italian thousand-lira notes. There was a letter among the notes, a penciled scrawl in French, and he read:

"I've found work and a place to live in a nearby village, but I wanted to see my mother and Rosalba again. Italian friends lent me some money to give to them, so that they could leave Argentera and go to Tuscany, where my mother has some relatives. I tried to cross the frontier twice, but police were guarding the pass. I had to lie low all night long to avoid them, and I had to give up any idea of getting back home. Then I thought that perhaps you, who know the mountains so well . . . Oh, I know it's a great deal to ask of you. I'll leave the money with you, since you've left your tools outside, and that means you will be coming back. I will try to come up to see you again in a week or so."

"Thank you for your friendship, and for believing in me.

Alberto."

Vincent felt bitterly disappointed as he finished reading the letter. Alberto had come and gone during his absence. But his disappointment gave way almost at once to quite another feeling. Alberto trusted him, thought of him as a man, and had asked him to undertake a serious mission. He was depending on him.

Vincent counted the banknotes. There were twenty-seven of them, and it seemed a great sum of money to him, almost a fortune. He put them in a wooden box he had made himself during those lost hours of work, and hid it in a corner of the hayloft. Then, before going to bed, he read through Alberto's letter again.

"Tomorrow I'll go and take them that money," he said aloud.

7

Another Mystery

ALBERTO said he had run right into the frontier guards: the man with the bandaged head had not lied. Young Deer Pass was sometimes guarded, and Vincent himself also ran the risk of an unwanted meeting. All the same, he could not keep the money, since Alberto had counted on him to get it to his mother and Rosalba. He had to go back to Argentera.

After much thought, he decided to go without Bichounette. It would be difficult to escape with her if he were taken by surprise. He would set out on foot, with Miski, whose feet made less noise than the mule's hoofs. Miski had a quick ear, and knew when to bark and when to be silent: the dog would be able to warn his master of danger.

It was settled, then. He would leave Wolf Ridge that evening, cross the frontier after dark, and reach Argentera before dawn. He would hide all day if necessary in Rosalba's house, and set out for home the following night. He must, of course, allow two good hours more on foot than when he took Bichounette, but the thought of the long night march did not worry him. He was strong; and his stout shoes with their rubber studs made no more noise than sandals.

All day long, stripped to the waist, he raked the hay, and thought of his departure. The hours seemed endless. At last the golden rays of the sun left the valley and slanted across the hills. As soon as the last load of fodder had been brought in, he filled his knapsack with the food he would need for the journey. The precious banknotes were hidden in the lining of his jacket, on the shoulder, where they replaced the shoulder-pad that he had taken out. He was ready.

"Let's go, Miski! And remember, no noise! Don't bark at the moon if it comes out!"

But there was little chance of the moon venturing to show its face before morning, since it was in its last quarter. The weather was ideal for such an expedition. Yet Vincent had a queer feeling as he left the hut, a sort of uneasiness he had not experienced that first time. Was it because the journey would be longer without Bichounette? Or because of the money he carried on him, and for which he was responsible? Or because of the Italian police?

Whatever it was, he knew he had to go, so he set out on his journey. One by one the tall peaks lost their crimson glow and retreated into the shadow, while overhead the sky was pricked with stars. It was going to be clear and cold, an excellent night for walking. Miski trotted along in front of Vincent, turning around from time to time to make sure that his master was following. The hut was already out of sight. They left Wolf Ridge for a track that could only just be seen, overlooking the Black Abyss. It would bring them out onto the path leading to Young Deer Pass.

The mountains were enfolded in such silence that Miski, who had never before been so high, seemed a little uneasy. Because of the night and the altitude the cold grew sharper. They walked for two long hours, until Young Deer Pass stood out clearly in the distance. They would reach it in less than an hour, if all went well. The landscape was completely different now. There were no more firs, no more vegetation, no moss, nothing but a chaotic mass of tumbled rocks, their dark shapes looking like a great herd of elephants.

Instinctively, Miski drew near his master, and lifted his head from time to time, hoping to hear his voice. Vincent thought of Argentera, of the money he was carrying, of Rosalba.

Vincent and Miski came to a sudden halt.

The total silence had been shattered abruptly by a stone that suddenly moved on the mountain, rolling down the slope, bouncing from one rock to another until it fell into a ravine. Alerted,

Miski stood like a hunting dog, one leg raised.

"It's nothing, Miski, only a stone."

He had not even finished speaking when another stone came clattering down in a shower of gravel that bounced off the rocks. Was there going to be a landfall?

"Don't let's stay here, Miski, let's get out!"

But the dog refused to follow him. He stood like a statue in the middle of the path, his ears pointed in the direction from which the stones seemed to have fallen.

"Come on, Miski!"

Vincent went quickly back to seize him by the collar, but Miski, his eyes still riveted to the same spot, began to quiver and bared his fangs. Vincent knew the dog well enough to be able to interpret these signs. Miski had seen something more, something other than stones—an ibex perhaps? or a chamois?

In his turn, the mountain lad looked about him, and his heart suddenly began to beat faster. He had caught sight of a shadow up there among the rocks, a curious shadow wider and less agile than that of an ibex or chamois, curiously like that of a man. He tried to hold the dog back, but he was too late; the animal had already bounded forward. Jumping from one rock to the next, gliding into crevices, slipping on the loose stones, Miski had every intention of overtaking the shadow.

"Here, Miski!"

Vincent lost sight of him almost at once, but he could hear his panting breath, and the crunching of the stones that rolled beneath his feet.

"Here, Miski!"

Then the noises grew fainter, though the rattling of stones from time to time showed that Miski was still in pursuit of the shadow. Vincent waited anxiously, holding his breath. All at once he heard the baying of his dog, like a cry of distress, and then nothing but the vast and melancholy silence of the heights. What had happened? Had Miski fallen into a ravine, bewildered by the darkness? Was he wounded?

Horror-stricken, Vincent listened hard, hoping for a new and reassuring outburst of barking.

"Come back, Miski, come back!"

Two minutes, then three went by. Vincent's fears became unendurable. At last he set off among the frightening masses of tumbled rock, where hollows were still filled with ice and snow. He was soon out of breath, and he could very easily have broken an arm or a leg as he clambered over the rocks, stopping only to get his breath back or to listen.

"Miski, where are you?"

He went on scrambling in the direction he believed the last spattering of stones had come from.

"Miski! Miski!"

Then at last a faint bark answered him. He

went on climbing with renewed vigor, streaming with sweat in spite of the cold, and now and again taking the risk of pointing his flashlight ahead as he went, to save time. Then all at once he cried out:

"Oh!"

There was Miski stretched full length at the foot of a great mass of rock. He leapt down and tried to lift up his faithful companion. The dog uttered a muffled cry of pain, and the boy felt something warm trickling over his hands.

"Blood! You are hurt."

Vincent examined the poor animal by the light of his lamp. The flesh had been cut open near the shoulder by something sharp, and the wound was bleeding freely. Gently he tried to find out whether the shoulder joint could be moved. Miski uttered a louder protest, but did not howl, so it seemed that the leg was not broken. Vincent made a dressing with his handkerchief, and fixed it securely round the shoulder with his belt. One thing was certain, Miski had not received that wound by falling among the rocks. Such a fall would have bruised him, knocked him out, or broken his bones: but none of these rocks was so sharp-edged that it would have slashed open his shoulder. The animal had been attacked with a knife, an extremely sharp knife. The shadow that moved upon the mountain had in fact been a man, but Vincent could not understand how Miski, so strong and so alert, had allowed himself to be attacked.

The explanation suddenly occurred to Vincent. The man, realizing that the dog would catch up with him, must have hidden behind this very rock, pretending to be dead. When Miski arrived in hot pursuit, and started to sniff the inert body, the man must have struck out brutally with his knife and then run off at once across the loose stones.

Vincent was trembling as much as his dog.

He was seized by an aftermath of terror, in case the man was still in hiding near them, however unlikely that might be. So he began to look all around the great rock with his light, in an attempt to overcome this terror.

Only a few feet from Miski he came upon a length of rope, not neatly coiled, but in a tangle, as though it had fallen from a bag and unwound on the ground. It was a long rope, like the ones used on the farms to tie down the hay on the haycarts, but the odd thing about this one was that it was knotted at intervals, and one end was furnished with an iron hook. It puzzled him, and he wondered what the man could possibly want with such a rope. He coiled it, and stuffed it into his knapsack, after which he searched the rest of the ground nearby, but without making any further discovery.

He went back to Miski, who was still whimpering softly. He was just about to lift the dog when he caught sight of something gleaming in the light of the lamp he had placed on the ground.

He picked it up quickly, and examined it closely. It was a big leather button mounted on metal, the sort that came from a shepherd's coat or a thick windbreaker. Suddenly he gave a start.

"This button! . . ." Yes, it was the Italian at Argentera who had the same, sewn on his heavy jacket. Was he then the man who had struck Miski down so savagely before he fled into the night?

Vincent stared at the button and tried to work things out, but Miski was in pain and he must get going. He lifted him across his shoulders, the way the people of Lauzière bring injured sheep back from the mountain, and set out for the path. The dog whined with pain at every false step, every jolt, until at last they reached the track again. With infinite care, Vincent put his heavy burden down, so that he could get his breath back. Just for a moment, he looked up at Young Deer Pass, so very near. But there was nothing he could do, he knew he had to give up, and tears of frustration came into his eyes.

Dawn was just beginning to touch the peaks with glimmering whiteness when Vincent reached the hut, so exhausted that he could no longer walk straight. Miski was such a weight across his shoulders that he'd been forced to rest more than ten times on the journey back. And all the time Miski, parched through loss of blood, had panted as though he had run a des-

perate race. As soon as they got back, the poor beast emptied three big bowls of fresh water, one after the other.

The young mountain boy took the kerosene lamp down from the ceiling, and looked closely at the dog's wounded shoulder. He removed the handkerchief as carefully as he could, for it was stuck to the hairs clotted with dried blood. The blade of the knife had gashed the skin and cut into the flesh to a depth of about four inches, but by a miracle it had not touched the bone. Miski submitted quietly to the cleansing of his painful wound, realizing that it was for his own good.

"My poor Miski, you really have had a narrow escape! If only you could speak, and tell me what happened!"

He put on another dressing, made from a clean rag, and strapped it tight so as to close the wound, and then made the dog comfortable on the floor beside the stove, which he had relit.

With the pain eased, and reassured by the voice and presence of his master, the animal closed his eyes and went to sleep.

At last, in the peace of the hut, Vincent had time to think about the vicious attack that had nearly cost the life of his dog. There was no doubt at all that the attacker was that Italian from Argentera, but what was he doing over on the French side again? Was he seeking out accomplices to whom he had given the cross?

Looking for money? Why had he turned aside among those tumbled rocks, with the risk of breaking his legs in the total darkness, instead of keeping to the track? Had he caught sight of Vincent in the distance, and was that why? And what was that knotted rope for?

Vincent examined it carefully under the light of the lamp, which he had hung from the ceiling again. At first he thought it might be a mountaineering rope, till he remembered that mountaineers never used knotted ropes, since theirs must slide freely; nor could he discover the purpose of the big iron hook at the end, which had not been bought, but had quite obviously been made crudely by hand.

Apart from his certainty that the man was the one he had met in Argentera, the mystery was as great as ever. Worn out, and finding no answer to any of his questions, Vincent stretched out on his bunk, and in spite of all his troubling thoughts, he too fell asleep, like Miski.

8

So Near the Goal

WHEN he awoke, the midday sun was burnishing Wolf Ridge. He had slept like a log for seven hours, and now his first thought was for Miski. The dog was exactly as he had left him, near the stove, and he did not seem to be in too much pain. He wagged his tail and tried to get up to greet his master, but one of his legs gave way, and he fell back onto the floor. Vincent brought him some more water. His nose was hot, a sign that he was running a temperature.

"Poor old Miski! I wish we knew what that man was doing up there."

The dressing had slipped, and he set to work to make another. The wound was no longer bleeding, and it looked as though it was already closing.

"Just be patient, Miski. It will soon heal up."

For about the twentieth time, Vincent tried to work out the meaning of what had happened. He wondered whether the man had simply been afraid of the dog, or whether he would have made the same use of his knife had it been Vincent who caught up with him and not Miski.

That was a horrible thought. He tried to make himself believe that the button was a very ordinary one, and the man only a smuggler who thought he was being chased by a police dog, and so had done the only thing he could to get away from the animal. But he could not deceive himself for long. There was no doubt at all that the man was the one he knew, and the most Vincent could do to cheer himself up was to suppose that the man had left the path for fear of the Italian police, who were at present guarding the frontier, and not because of himself or his dog.

Though he was very much afraid and discouraged, and fully aware of the danger, Vincent could think of nothing but his next attempt to reach Argentera. Rosalba needed the money, and he could not get her out of his mind.

He must set out again, but he did not know when he would be able to go. He could not take Miski with him now, nor could he leave the dog alone in the hut. He thought of Gilles, who had promised to come up the moment he was called. He would give the agreed signal that very night, so that Gilles could be there the next morning, and he himself ready to set out again the following night.

Glad to have reached a decision, and feeling

reassured about it all once more, he set to work again, cutting the grass with fierce sweeping movements of his scythe. It was as though he were avenging Miski's wound by taking it out on the grasslands.

Toward the middle of the afternoon, the sky, wonderfully clear all morning, became overcast. One after the other the high peaks and Young Deer Pass were swallowed up by the clouds that overhung the hollows like thick layers of cottonwool. Wolf Ridge in its turn was enveloped in a "fat" mist, as it was called in the region, and isolated from the rest of the world.

Vincent returned to the hut in a worried frame of mind, desperately hoping that, as the air grew colder in the course of the evening, the mist would be driven toward the heights, as it sometimes was. But unfortunately, the mist was still there, thick as smoke, at the time when he should have been waving his lantern. There was no visibility a hundred feet from the hut, and neither the lantern nor the pocket flashlight would be able to pierce that thick curtain. It was impossible to get in touch with Gilles.

The evening seemed endless to Vincent. He spent it near Miski, who was less feverish than in the morning, and went to bed early, although he found it difficult to get to sleep. Nightmares came to trouble him. He saw the precious banknotes blowing away in the mountain wind, and when he ran to catch them, he fell among the rocks and the notes were swept farther away.

The following day, as soon as he woke up, he ran to the hayloft where he had hidden the wooden box. The notes were all there. Outside, the weather was still gray, but the cloud ceiling had lifted to the level of Young Deer Pass.

"Let's hope the mist doesn't come down again," he said to himself.

He looked after Miski, who was better, and took some food. The day seemed even longer than the one before. At last, about half-past eight, afraid of being late for his rendezvous with Gilles, he went out onto Wolf Ridge and waved his lantern several times at arm's length. At exactly five to nine he saw a pinpoint of light from a flashlight answering him from the direction of the stone bridge. His friend had been faithful to their arrangement.

"He'll be here midday tomorrow, that's certain."

He went back to the hut and his nightmares of the previous evening came suddenly into his mind. He knew that the money would torment him until he had delivered it.

"What's the point of waiting until tomorrow night? I could set off now. Miski's much better. He won't need anything tonight."

Vincent made up his mind then and there. He packed his knapsack again, got the money

and put it back carefully in the shoulder of his jacket. After making sure that Bichounette's tether was not so long that she could get strangled in it, he filled a dish with soup and placed it near Miski. Then he settled himself at a corner of the table, and wrote a note for his friend to read when he arrived:

"Dear Gilles,

I have to go back to Argentera. I'm leaving tonight. I leave Miski in your charge—he got hurt yesterday on the mountain. All you need do is give him a new dressing of clean rag which you'll find in the chest. Bichounette on the other hand doesn't need anything. Just untie her and let her graze around the hut. Don't worry about me. I don't know when I'll be back. I'll have a lot to tell you. I'm very hopeful.

Thank you,
Vincent."

He placed the note in a prominent position on the table, stroked Miski for the last time and told him not to move, nor to pull at the dressing with his fangs. Then he went out, leaving the door unlocked.

The weather was still overcast, and there was not a single star in the sky. The moon would not come out until early morning, for which he was glad. He made certain that the wad of notes was still in place and then, alpenstock in hand, he hurried off.

Two hours later he reached the place where the path went across that mass of tumbled rock. He could not prevent a moment of dread, and a cold shiver ran down his back as he quickened his step. But there was nothing there, the mountain was deserted. He reached Young Deer Pass just after midnight, and found it swept by an icy wind that froze him through, a treacherous wind carrying snowflakes. He grew anxious again, and stopped to listen and to peer into the darkness. There might be guards patrolling the border, as there had been when Alberto tried to cross it.

All was quiet, however, so he began the long and steep descent into the Italian valley. He knew the hairpin bends, and the dangerous parts. He followed the twists of the path for a long time without coming to the place where the fir trees grew. But he was not alarmed. Another hour, and he would be in Argentera. As soon as the first houses came into sight, he would leave the road and skirt the village. He would cross the torrent lower down, and avoid using the bridge by jumping across the rocks that littered the river bed now that the water was low. From there he could reach the house with the red shutters.

He felt that these plans were foolproof. Already he saw himself putting the precious banknotes on the table. With them Rosalba and her mother could get away from this region that had grown so unfriendly toward them. There was always the chance, of course, that things had happened since his last visit; discoveries might have been made that no longer pointed to Alberto's guilt. But however matters stood, he had made up his mind to tell Rosalba about the man with the bandaged head, who would certainly be known to her. He would tell her, too, about the adventure in Young Deer Pass, about the rope and the button he had found.

He was thinking of all this as he walked along the path, which was wider now, and not so stony. The odd thing was that the nearer he came to Argentera, the safer he felt. If he had been fated to encounter the police, it would have been higher up, in the pass.

The air, so cold in the pass, had become almost warm again. Already he thought he could see the square belltower of the church at Argentera standing out in the distance and the darkness.

Then he came to a bend in the road, and stopped abruptly. About twenty feet ahead there was a shadow in the middle of the path. He gulped in surprise, turned around and began to run as fast as he could back up the path again, so as to get away. He had only gone about three hundred yards when another shadow appeared in front of him. He came to a halt, panic-stricken, his heart thudding, looking desperately for some way of escape. Huge piled rocks formed a high wall on his right: on his left was the precipice. He had fallen into a trap. There was no escape.

"The money . . . I must . . . oh, quick . . ."

He wanted to hide the notes under a stone, under anything, but it was too late: the two shadows had already caught up with him. He saw by their green uniforms, and the plumes in their hats, that they were Italian policemen. He was blinded by the light of a powerful flashlight.

"Were you hoping to get away?"

He stayed stock still, his mouth set, his body tensed.

"Where d'you come from? You've just come through the pass, haven't you?"

He was afraid of giving Alberto away.

"I got lost on the mountain. I live in France, near the frontier, in a summer hut."

"Nobody goes off for a walk like that, in the middle of the night. Where are your papers?"

He shook his head without speaking..

"Come on now, speak up. What were you intending to do in Argentera?"

He hesitated, well aware that he would not be able to go on lying. After all, he had done nothing wrong, so why not tell the truth straight out?

"I came to see Alberto Conti's mother and sister." At these words the policemen pricked up their ears.

"Alberto Conti? . . . The man who stole the

gold cross of Santa Anna? . . . You know him?"

Vincent remained silent for a moment, but it was pretty certain that everyone in Argentera knew that Alberto had fled into France, and since he was safe on the other side of the frontier. . . .

"The other night Alberto Conti came knocking at my hut. He wanted to see his mother and sister again, to see how they were getting on, but he didn't dare come back. So I came instead of him."

The two men, skeptical, shook their heads.

"And what've you got in there?"

Vincent slipped off the straps of his knapsack.

"Only some food for the journey; you can see for yourselves."

But the Italians were not satisfied. Vincent remembering the money, could not help shivering. They began to search him by turning out his pockets: his trousers first, and then his jacket. Afterwards they went methodically over every possible hiding place, the cuffs of his trousers, the seams of all his clothing. They turned his collar up and felt it, then passed along his shoulder, while Vincent tried not to give himself away. He felt a hand lingering, leaning hard, then pressing down upon the shoulder-pad of his jacket.

"What are you hiding there?"

The hand withdrew the wad of notes. The policemen looked closely at them and counted

them rapidly by the light of the flashlight. Then
Vincent saw the money disappear into a pocket.
He wanted to protest, but he had only just
enough courage left to stop himself from burst-
ing into tears. The two men, who had become
much sterner, pushed him along in front of
them.

"Right! Now we understand . . . Get going!"

He made no attempt to resist. The policemen
walked behind in silence, then began to talk
to each other in Italian. Vincent could not understand what they said; he could only recognize
the name Santa Anna, which they repeated
several times over.

"Come on! *Presto!* Faster!"

He could not stop himself from slowing down.
Where were they taking him? What were they
going to do with him? Surely they would soon
let him explain matters; they couldn't arrest him
as a thief.

It was not yet dawn, but it soon would be.
Now he could just see Argentera, the church,
the village, the bridge. He recognized the little
house with the red shutters, and had a violent
desire to escape. What was the good? He would
be caught again at once.

The path had turned into a fairly wide road,
and the policemen were now walking one on
each side of their prisoner. As the small group
entered the center of the village, an old man,
out early to fetch water from the fountain,

stopped and crossed himself as though to chase away evil spirits. Vincent felt desperately ashamed of being treated as a thief when he had done nothing wrong.

The policemen stopped outside a house not very different from the others, except that it was a little larger. Above the door was the word MUNICIPO, the Town Hall. Vincent was taken into a small, low-ceilinged room that smelled of tobacco, and at first he was dazzled by the lamp that had just been lit. The policemen took off their plumed hats, put their revolvers on a rack and locked the money in a drawer. Then they settled themselvs at a desk piled with papers, lit cigars and at last turned to Vincent.

"Your name?"

"Vincent Missilier."

"Age?"

"I'm fourteen."

The two Italians looked him over from head to heel with sardonic eyes.

"Sure you're not older? You're nearly as tall and as broad as a man."

"I was fourteen on the seventeenth of April, honestly."

"Where do your parents live?"

"Just the other side of the frontier, at Lauzière —but for the last six weeks I've been living by myself in the hut, haymaking."

One of the policemen was writing Vincent's replies in a book. The other, the smaller one who seemed to be in charge, frowned suddenly.

"Now I'm warning you, don't start telling fibs! Where did that money come from and what were you going to do with it?"

Some time back, while he was walking along in front of the two policemen, Vincent had been able to get a grip on himself, and to think of some explanation for the money. He realized at once how difficult it would be to lie about it, and he had decided that the simplest thing to do would be to tell the truth.

"I told you that Alberto Conti was worried about his mother and sister. He was afraid that the people in the village would turn nasty. He went to some Italian friends in France, and they lent him the money so that his family could leave

Argentera. I came through Young Deer Pass to bring them the money."

The man listened, puffing away at his cigar. "Really? Couldn't you have thought up a better story?"

Vincent stiffened.

"If you only knew how unhappy Alberto was when I saw him! I'm sure he's not guilty. I know he didn't steal the cross of Santa Anna. You must give that money back to me, and I must take it to Rosalba and her mother. They need it."

The two men looked at each other, exchanging a smile.

"Go on!"

"I've told you the truth, and there's nothing else to say."

There was a long and heavy silence. Then the man in charge stubbed out his half-smoked cigar in an ashtray, got up, and came to stand in front of Vincent.

"Is that really all you've got to say? And do you really think we'd swallow a yarn like that?"

The boy grew angry.

"It's not a yarn! It's the truth!"

"That's enough! You'd do better to tell us straight off just how much this Alberto Conti paid you."

Vincent's eyes grew wide with astonishment. "How much he . . . ?"

"Don't pretend you don't understand. You

know what I mean all right. Nobody would go through Young Deer Pass in the middle of the night like that without some little recompense, eh?"

"Alberto didn't give me anything. . . . Nor would I have accepted anything. And anyway the money isn't his; he borrowed it."

The two men shook with laughter.

"Oh, sure, it's borrowed money! This Alberto coached you well and you believe him—or pretend to! What d'you take us for? Alberto has managed to sell the gold cross, but since he daren't set foot in Italy again—and for a very good reason—he got you to do the job for him!"

"Oh, no!"

"Oh, yes, it's an old dodge. What's more, he certainly got more than twenty-seven thousand lire for the gold cross. Your journey was just a trial trip: you can be sure he'd have asked you to go again."

This time Vincent understood what they were accusing him of. "It isn't true," he answered with indignation. "I swear Alberto didn't give me anything. This money doesn't come from the cross of Santa Anna. . . . Alberto is not guilty!"

"No? After the proof you've brought us?"

He was outraged by these accusations, against which he could do nothing. Suddenly he lifted his head. He had remembered the man who fled into the snow and who had wounded Miski; he remembered the rope and the lost button.

He longed to voice his own suspicions, make his own accusations. But the words stuck in his throat. Suspicions are not proof, and everything he had seen had happened on the French side of the frontier, so that the Italian police couldn't care less. And if it turned out that the man with the bandaged head had been wrongly accused, he would be in even greater trouble; for the man would deny everything.

It was all over and he had nothing more to say.

Completely overwhelmed, he let himself be led into the passage and pushed into a small room rather like a cell, where the daylight entered through a high barred window. It was furnished only with a mattress on the floor, and a stool. Behind him the door closed, creaking, a key turned in the lock, a bolt slid home. He was a prisoner.

9

The Keys

AS soon as he was alone, Vincent dropped on to the mattress, seized by a terrible despair. Before the police, he had tried to keep his courage up. But now, between four bare walls, with no one watching, he gave free rein to his misery. So Alberto had deceived him. The money that he, Vincent, had brought with never a moment's doubt, had come from the cross of Santa Anna. And that made Rosalba's brother the most two-faced, the most cunning of evildoers.

When Vincent was facing them, he had cried out in anger against the police. Then gradually, stealthily, he had been assailed by doubt, and there is nothing worse than doubt.

But the police *must* be wrong, they did not know. Alberto's tears, the tears of a desperately unhappy man, were real tears, like Rosalba's.

Vincent sat there on the mattress, trying to wipe out of his mind the terrible accusations the police had made.

"If only I could see Rosalba," he thought, "I

know I could read the truth in her eyes."

It was now dawn. Gradually, as night drew to its end, the weather had cleared. Through the little window placed high in the wall just beneath the ceiling, he could see a square of clear sky, and in one corner the distant peak of a mountain. Then he thought of Lauzière. His parents would be told: he wondered what his father would say, and his mother. Would they too believe that he was the accomplice of a thief?

A long time went by. Seven o'clock sounded from the nearby bell-tower. Utterly worn out, his head aching, he stretched out on the mattress, and though he tried to keep awake, he fell heavily asleep.

When he opened his eyes again, after terrible nightmares, he noticed that someone had been in while he slept, and had put a bowl of soup and a hunk of bread on the stool. As soon as he saw them, he realized how hungry he was. The soup was still hot, and yellow with saffron. He tasted it and found that it was good. The bread was good, too, neither black nor stale like the bread that was given to prisoners in books. Feeling much better, he got up and climbed onto the stool, to try to see out the window; but it was too high up. The sun too seemed very high, and he wondered what the time was. The bells of the tower answered him by sounding twice. Had he slept on as long as that? He began worrying again about what the police would do to him, and wondering whether his parents had been told by now.

He was still standing in front of the little window when the sound of steps in the passage made him turn around. He expected to see one of the policemen, but he found himself facing instead a fat man with a huge paunch, nearly bald, and in his shirtsleeves.

"I came to see if you were still asleep, if your soup was cold. . . . You've eaten it all? Are you still hungry?"

Vincent shook his head, and looked questioningly at the man, who explained:

"I'm the caretaker of the Town Hall, and the warder of the prison cell as well . . . it's not often used, thank goodness. It's the first time anyway that they've brought me a prisoner as young as you."

The Italian was obviously all ready for a chat. He sat down comfortably on the straw mattress.

"The police told me. . . . Aren't you ashamed, at your age?"

Vincent drew himself up.

"I haven't done anything. I told the truth, but no one will believe me."

The good-natured warder wagged his head sympathetically.

"You look decent enough, I must say . . . but, my poor boy, you're in a fine mess, aren't you?"

"What are they going to do with me?"

"Take you to Sallega, because here, as you can see, it's not a real prison. You'll be questioned again when you get there."

"Sallega," Vincent said after him. "Is it far?"

"About seven and a half miles from here, in the valley bottom. It's the county seat."

"Have my parents been told yet?"

"Not yet. I'm in charge of the phone, and so far the police have only asked to be put through to Sallega. . . . But you can be sure they'll be told quite soon now, from there."

The caretaker swung his key as he spoke, a rusty key that did not look as though it was often used. Then he put it in his pocket so that he could mop his face, for it was hot in the locked room.

"If you'd like some air," he offered, "I could open the window."

He got to his feet with some difficulty, went out, and came back with a broom, using the handle to open the window. Then, when he had mopped his face again, he went out, locking the door behind him, and pushing the bolt in place.

Vincent went to stand under the high window to get a little fresh air: his head was aching badly. So at any moment now the police were coming to take him to a real prison, where he would be questioned again. He could add nothing to what he had already said. If only he could see Rosalba and talk to her, before he left.

He sat down again on the mattress. Four

o'clock sounded from the tower, then five. Why were the police waiting so long? At seven, footsteps sounded in the corridor: he rose to his feet, trembling. The door opened: it was the warder again.

"Orders countermanded," he boomed, in his resonant voice that sounded as though it came out of a barrel. "You'll be spending the night here. The road to Sallega is blocked—two big fir trees have fallen across it. The phone's cut off too. You won't lose anything by staying here. My wife's a good cook, and you'll have the same food as we do."

Vincent was not interested in good cooking. But the thought that he would not be leaving that night, and that his family would not have been told, since the phone was cut off, did cheer him up a little. It only put things off for a while, of course, but anything might happen in the meantime.

The evening slowly drew to an end. The sun, which at that hour of the day would still be burnishing Wolf Ridge, had already left the Italian slopes.

Soon the caretaker returned, carrying a large bowl of steaming soup, and wishing his prisoner good appetite as he placed it on the stool. It smelled as good as the other, but Vincent had to force himself to swallow it. When he had finished it he went back to the open window, through which came evening sounds. A few villagers came to the fountain and gossiped there: and he found himself listening hard, hoping to hear Rosalba's voice.

Then the noises grew less frequent, and the square corner of sky became dark. Nine o'clock sounded from the tower: night had fallen.

"If only I could get away!" The thought came suddenly into Vincent's mind. He walked around his cell, fingered the lock, and felt around a spyhole cut in the door. The small wooden trap that sealed it and which worked from the outside was not fastened. He pushed it open and put his arm through, groping for the bolt, but he could not find it: it must be fixed lower down. He went back to the window. He could not reach it even if he climbed onto the stool. It would not have helped much anyway; the four bars guarding it seemed to be fixed securely. It really looked as though escape were out of the question.

He stretched out on the mattress, listening to the slow passing of the hours. The village was now completely deserted. Just as eleven o'clock sounded from the tower, he heard a strange noise that made him jump, a sharp metallic sound as though something iron had knocked against one of the bars at the window.

He rose quickly to his feet, staring up at it, but he could see nothing. He knew, however, that he had not been mistaken: something had certainly knocked against one of the bars.

He kept on looking up at the window, his eyes fixed on the dim light coming through. Then he jumped a second time; for he heard the same noise again, and this time he saw something hooked onto one of the bars at the bottom. He stood listening for a while, expecting to hear the sound of footsteps outside, but there was nothing. So he climbed onto the stool and stood on the very tips of his toes. When he saw what was around the bar, his heart began to race.

"Keys!"

Who could have thrown him these keys, so that he could break out? Rosalba? Yes, it could only be she. She must have heard talk in the village about the young boy the police had caught on the road through Young Deer Pass. Of course she would have realized at once who it was, and that he had come back again to see her. He was so overjoyed that he could not move. Now if only he could get them. . . . He stretched up as high as he could against the wall to reach the keys, but it was no use. Then he remembered the broom the caretaker had forgotten to take away after he had opened the window. He tried to make the keys fall into his cell by poking at them with the end of the broomstick, but unfortunately they had gotten caught around the bar, and the least false movement would make them drop outside. He decided to make sure that Rosalba was still there close to the wall, before he risked any clumsy

movement. She could send them up for the third time if he failed to get them in. He whispered:

"Who's there?"

Then, a little louder:

"Rosalba, is it you?"

No answer came to disturb the silence of the night. Rosalba had not dared stay longer, or else she had not noticed that the bunch of keys had lodged in the bars. Patiently he struggled to release the precious keys; but it was all a waste of time, for the round wooden handle and the soft bristles of the broom offered nothing to grip with. He realized that if he went on trying he would only succeed in pushing the keys outside.

It was then he thought of taking the broom apart. The handle was loose, anyway. Using the soles of his shoes as a vise, he succeeded in pulling out the nail that held the broom to the stick; then he fixed it at the end of the handle so as to make a sort of hook. After a few fumbling attempts, he managed to draw the keys toward him and they fell to the floor. He almost shouted with joy.

There were about twenty keys in the bunch, all different shapes and sizes. Where had Rosalba found them? Had someone given them to her? Then he saw that the biggest one had a piece of paper rolled around it and tied with thread. He removed it carefully, and unrolled it. But it was too dark in the cell to read the message, or even make out a few letters.

Oh well, the important thing at the moment was to get out. He quickly stuffed the paper into his pocket, and looked over the keys, comparing them in his mind with the one he had seen in the caretaker's hands. Most of them were too small; there were only about three or four that seemed possible. He tried them one after the other, without making a sound. Two went in easily, but would not turn the lock. Perhaps this was a very special and complicated lock; and yet the key that the caretaker had been twisting in his hands had seemed to him an ordinary one. He tried once more, forced the key to the right, then to the left. Just as he was about to give up, the lock was suddenly released.

He heaved a great sigh of relief. There was still the bolt, however. He stretched his arm through the spyhole and began groping again with the help of the broom handle to discover its position. He found it easily, but it was impossible to undo it. It must be an old one, rusty like the key, and difficult to move. He tried it several times, and in the end risked hitting it a bit to make it work. It was impossible to do all this without making a noise, and he was terrified when the fanlight above the door suddenly showed a light. Had the caretaker heard?

He quickly shut the spyhole, hid the dismantled broom under the mattress, and then stretched out on it, pretending to be asleep. Ten minutes went by, and there was still no sound of stealthy footsteps in the passage. He got up and pushed the spyhole open. There was no light anymore. He waited a while, to make quite sure, then applied himself once more to his task. It was extremely difficult: he could only use one arm, and he couldn't see what he was doing. At last the bolt slid back.

His heart constricted with excitement and terror, he pushed the door open, lifting it on its hinges a little so that it would not creak. The passage was plunged in total darkness. Only a small rectangle that was not quite so dark betrayed the fanlight over the outside door. He crept stealthily forward. The front door, too, would certainly be locked. He fumbled for the lock, and found that luck was with him. The careless caretaker had left the key in the lock. Vincent was free.

10

Rendezvous in the Night

THE village was deserted and drowned in darkness. The only light came from an electric bulb above the fountain in the middle of the Square.

Vincent ran across the empty space, and crouched against the stone basin, so as to merge with it.

Then quickly, with trembling fingers, he drew from his pocket the paper he had found wrapped round the key. He smoothed it out beneath the light, and was struck by the writing—big, badly formed printed letters. He made out:

"I'm waiting for you by the split rock on the road to Young Deer Pass.

Rosalba."

He was in a hurry to leave this spot, too well lighted by the lamp, so he read the note quickly again to memorize the words, then ran across the Square once more to hide himself in an angle of the wall.

"On the road to the pass," he repeated. "By the split rock."

He knew the rock, a great section of the mountain with a wide crack in it that looked as though it had been made by a giant's sword. It was near the place where the police had arrested him. Why had Rosalba chosen a meeting place so far from the village? Had she been afraid to fix some nearer place—the thicket behind her house, for instance? And then, why was the message printed as if she wanted to disguise her handwriting, when she had not hesitated to put her own name to it?

All this seemed very odd to him, but he had no time to think it over. Eleven o'clock had sounded a long time ago, and he could not expect her to wait the whole night through. Keeping to the walls, he came to the end of the village, and had just set out on the road to the pass when he came to a halt, struck by a sudden uneasiness. An idea had just come into his mind.

"If Rosalba is waiting there for me, her mother must surely have stayed behind, since she was so ill the other day. Rosalba will have told her everything . . . I ought to go and see her."

He went back on his tracks, still hugging the walls, and ready all the time to go into hiding at the least sign of danger. In spite of the dark, he recognized without any difficulty the little house with the red shutters, sleeping like the rest. He knocked at the door, gently at first, then a little more loudly. No one answered. There was nothing surprising about that, since the bedroom was upstairs. So he threw pebbles against the shutters on the upper story, waited a few moments, and then threw some more. He was about to throw yet another handful, even at the risk of rousing the neighbors, when he thought he saw a slender ray of light at the joining of the shutters. Rosalba's mother had heard him, and she must have gotten out of bed to look through the narrow crack. In a low voice he called:

"This is Vincent . . . Rosalba's friend."

He thought he heard a whisper, but almost at the same moment the light went out. Had Rosalba's mother, terrified because she had not recognized him, closed the window and put out the light? He stood there not knowing what to do, not daring to call out again for fear of attracting attention. Then, without warning the door was half opened. He was so astonished that his legs nearly gave way under him.

"Rosalba—you?"

The girl hardly recognized him, he looked so strange.

He came in, shaking all over, never taking his eyes off Rosalba, as though to make sure it was really she.

"Oh Vincent, what has happened? Something terrible . . . my brother . . . ?"

He shook his head, unable to speak. Drawing from his pocket the paper that had been rolled around the key, he held it out to her. She scanned it quickly, and then looked questioningly at Vincent.

"I don't understand."

"Didn't you write that message?"

She shook her head. He drew out the bunch of keys that were pulling his pocket out of shape.

"Then who sent me these master-keys?"

Rosalba's eyes filled with terror, as though she were suddenly afraid that Vincent had gone out of his mind.

"I still don't understand."

Vincent sank into a chair, unable to get out a single word. Rosalba knelt in front of him, so as to see his face, and took his hands in hers.

"Oh, do explain!"

There was a long silence. At last he lifted his head.

"You don't know, then, that the police arrested me last night on Young Deer Pass and shut me up in a cell in the Town Hall? I've just got out."

"The police? They arrested you? No, I didn't know. My mother is too afraid to go out anymore, and I left the house early this morning just to do the shopping, and to bring water from the fountain. I didn't meet anyone."

Then she added: "So that's why we received a summons this afternoon to go to Sallega tomorrow. The caretaker at the Town Hall brought it, and we were wondering what they wanted with us now."

There was a silence, and then came a slight sound from the room above, as though someone were turning over in bed.

"My mother didn't hear the stones you threw against the shutters. She doesn't like sleeping in the room looking on to the street anymore. Be careful not to wake her; she'd be terrified if she heard voices. Why did you come back to Argentera, Vincent? Have you seen Alberto again?"

"No, I didn't see your brother again, Rosalba.

As bad luck would have it, he returned to the hut on Wolf Ridge while I was down in the valley. He wanted to come back here to bring you some money, but he couldn't make it."

"Money? What money?"

"He wanted you to get out of this region now that you're so unhappy here. He'd borrowed twenty-seven thousand lire from some friends. I was bringing the money to you in his place. But the police took it from me. They believed it had come from the sale of the cross of Santa Anna."

As he finished speaking, he lowered his head, for he felt that he was somehow to blame in having allowed himself to be captured.

All at once he grew pale. For a few moments, sheltered by the little house with the red shutters, delighted to be seeing Rosalba again, he had forgotten the curious message.

"Look, Rosalba, since you knew nothing about this, who was it who arranged to meet me by the split rock? And who do these keys belong to, since you didn't send them to me?"

She took the keys, looked them over carefully, and thought for a moment.

"I do know that my brother had a bunch like these. He often used to repair locks in the village."

"Are his keys still here?"

"I expect so."

"Where did he keep them?"

"In the courtyard, I think, in the shed where we keep everything we don't need in the house."

"Let's go and see!"

Rosalba shivered at the thought of going out into the yard in the middle of the night, but she lit a candle all the same. Just as a precaution, Vincent surrounded the flame with a rough shade made out of a piece of cardboard, so that the light could not easily be seen. He saw that the shed was cluttered up with all sorts of odds and ends, tools, sacks of plaster and cement.

"Oh!" All at once Rosalba pointed to a nail sticking out of a beam. "I remember now—he used to hang them there, and they're not there now."

Vincent stared at the nail, then turned to Rosalba.

"Someone came here to get the keys and throw them to me in that cell."

"I can't believe it! Who was it?"

Vincent made no reply. Taking the candle from her, he ran the light over the shelves.

"Tell me, Rosalba, did your brother leave the tiling hammer they found near the chapel in this shed, unlocked?"

"Yes, like all his tools."

"And his boots?"

"His old boots, yes, the ones he didn't wear anymore. He kept them to use the leather."

Vincent drew in a deep breath. Now there was no more doubt. The man who had taken the hammer and the books so as to throw suspicion on Alberto had come back to take the keys he knew he would find there. As he thought it over, Vincent shuddered.

"Let's go back, Rosalba!"

A horrifying thought had just come into his mind. "Rosalba," he said, and his voice was shaking, "the man who threw those keys to me didn't want to help me. . . . He wanted to get rid of me!"

"Vincent!"

"The rendezvous he gave me is just right for the purpose—the very place where the path runs to the edge of the ravine."

"How horrible! But why should he want to?"

Vincent turned it over in his mind.

"I think I know, Rosalba. If he'd pulled it off, and I'd been found dead in the ravine, everyone would have believed that I'd got out of prison with your help, and then been killed accidentally while I was trying to get away. And you and your mother would have been accused all over again of aiding and abetting a criminal."

Vincent went on with his thoughts. The unknown man wanted to kill him: there was surely a link here with the man who was so suspicious of him, though he did not know why.

"Rosalba," he said at length, "the man who set the police on to your brother is most certainly a man from Argentera, and someone you know quite well. Anyway, he knows your home all right—the fact that the shed is kept unlocked,
118

and everything that's in it. You didn't hear anyone walking about in the courtyard after nightfall, did you?"

"No."

"And there's no one you suspect?"

"Practically the whole village turn their backs on us now, but I don't know . . ."

Vincent hesitated, for he was unwilling to speak without proof, but he knew that he must.

"What do you think of the man who lives in the house with the tiled roof just above the village? I asked him the way to your house the other day. His head was bandaged, and his arm in a sling."

"You must mean Rapalli, who hurt himself cutting wood in the forest."

"Did your brother know him well?"

"Of course. For several years Rapalli and Alberto worked together."

"Did you never suspect him?"

"Oh, Vincent, why should I? Rapalli wasn't a very good worker, so my brother left him. But that's not a reason. . . . Why, he was the only one to come and see us when Alberto had to get out of the country!"

Involuntarily, Vincent clenched his fists. Suddenly he jumped, as the little clock on the chimneypiece struck two. Two hours from now it would be dawn: the caretaker would wake up and give the alarm.

"Rosalba, I must be off."

A flicker of terror came into her eyes. She

seized Vincent's hands and held them tightly in her own.

"No . . . not along that path where someone is waiting to kill you! Oh no, I won't let you! You can hide here in the cellar!"

"That won't be any good, Rosalba. The police will be here tomorrow; they'll search the house from top to bottom. . . . And then, over there on the other side of the mountain, my parents will have been told, and they might believe that I was dead and lost in the mountains."

"But, Vincent, what if you meet him on your way back?"

"Is there no other way of getting to the pass?"

"There's only the old track, the one that used to climb above the split rock before the new road was cut into the mountain. But it's not safe now; part of it has fallen away. Someone got killed there only two years ago. No, Vincent, you can't go that way!"

"Where does it start?"

"My brother showed me one day when we were out walking together, but you won't find it easily in the dark. It forks off from the new path about half an hour's walk from here, just after a bend in the road."

"I'll have to try it, whatever it's like."

Rosalba did not argue with him, for she knew that he was quite right when he said that he had to go.

"Well then, promise me that you'll be very

careful. And if you can't find the path, come back here. I shall stay up all night."

Defying her fear of the dark, she went out into the courtyard and brought back an old rucksack belonging to Alberto. She put all that remained of the bread into it, together with some cheese and some chocolate. As the moment of separation drew near, she could not hold back her tears.

"Vincent, how will I know whether you got back safely to Wolf Ridge, without any harm coming to you?"

"No harm will come to me, Rosalba. I always keep the little Santa Anna you gave me in my pocket and the police didn't take it from me. She'll look after me, and help us to clear Alberto."

"Clear Alberto! If only we could!"

They fell silent for a few moments. Then Vincent said, "I'll try to come again, Rosalba."

She squeezed his hand hard.

"No, Vincent, the police would only get hold of you again. . . . From now on they'll be prowling about the pass every day. You mustn't . . ."

She thought hard for a while.

"Listen, if I hear anything that may help us, I'll climb up as far as Young Deer Pass."

"You? Up there?"

"My legs are strong. My brother used to take me up there sometimes, to pick edelweiss . . . and if I met the police, they couldn't say anything to me, since I wouldn't be trying to leave our side of the pass."

"And how shall I know that you have come?"

She thought for a moment.

"I'll bring a message that I'll put in . . . look, I'll put it in this old spectacle case my mother doesn't use any more. Just tell me where to put it, since you know the pass so well."

"The frontier is marked by a loose post on the right of the path as you come from Argentera. What you can do is put the case under a stone, three paces to the right of the post—don't forget, three paces. As soon as I can I'll come back, and then I'll leave a message at the same spot."

They would be able to keep in touch with each other. This knowledge gave them fresh courage and assurance.

"Go quickly, now," Rosalba murmured. "I shall stay up for the rest of the night, thinking of you, and praying to Santa Anna."

Vincent went off into the night. Half past two sounded from the bell-tower. Already half past two! A dog barked in a yard. Vincent was anxious to leave the village behind. The clear sky would make his trek across the mountains easier, and help him to discover the beginning of the old path. In Rosalba's house he had felt almost safe: outside all his terrors crowded upon him once more. He turned around several times, sure that he was being followed, though he knew that the caretaker at the Town Hall must be sleeping like a log, and no alarm had yet been given.

He had passed the last houses on the outskirts of the village, and climbed up as far as Rapalli's place. He could not help a sudden shiver, wondering whether it was really Rapalli lying in wait for him up there. He halted for a moment by a low stone wall, to look around and listen. The house was as silent as all the others. So he continued on his way, on the alert all the time, his ears cocked and his eyes searching the darkness ahead for the start of the old path. Suddenly he was afraid that he had already gone past it and that the man who was waiting for him would all at once loom over him.

He dared not go on. Instead he went back on his tracks, and at last came upon a sort of track on his right, cluttered with stones. This must be the ancient pathway. He set out along it, forced into dangerous climbing all the time by the great blocks of rock that had fallen from the mountain.

"I must be careful to make no noise," he said to himself. "There must be no stones clattering down."

The path he was on rose more steeply than the other, and there was a moment when he felt as though his heart had stopped beating, for there was suddenly nothing but a large rock and empty space before him. He felt so dizzy that he threw himself flat on the rock. He must have bypassed the path somewhere and lost his way. He retraced his steps and, after a while got on to the path again, and once more began climbing the massive boulders.

Since branching off from the newer path, the track had taken him about six hundred feet up, so at present he must be somewhere above the split rock. The temptation to look down on the road to the pass so far below him and try to discover the identity of the man waiting there for him, became too much for him to suppress. Ignoring the waste of time and the possible danger, he stepped off the track, at the risk of being unable to find it again, and came to an enormous rock, flat as a flagstone. He was afraid of suddenly facing empty space, as he had done earlier, so he crept forward on his hands and knees, taking care not to send stones rattling down.

He stopped abruptly; he had come to the edge of the rock. An immensity of space opened out before him. But when he looked down he saw immediately below a narrow winding thread running closely along the rock face, easily discernible even in the darkness.

"The path!"

He crawled forward again, stretching out his neck to look as far as possible along that narrow strip.

There was no one on the road to the pass. He knew now, however, that he was immediately above the split rock. Perhaps the stranger, tired

of waiting, and seeing that the night was coming to an end, had gone. Or was he hidden in some dark corner, crouched ready to leap out on the one for whom he was lying in wait?

Vincent stretched out on the rock, so icy cold that it froze his stomach. His eyes fell on a small dark mass huddled beside a boulder. From where he was, it looked something like a ball balancing on the edge of the path. . . . But it had just moved and changed shape. The shape stretched out, grew taller and then moved with infinite care onto the path. It went down to the first bend, stopped, stayed there for a while blending with the rocks, then came back to its former place on the path.

All this lasted only a few seconds, but Vincent had been able to recognize Rapalli's silhouette.

The man no longer had his arm in a sling, nor his head bandaged; but his broad shoulders, his general bearing, and his way of walking were all unmistakable.

So it was Rapalli, as he had guessed, who had thrown the keys through the cell window. . . . But why did the man want to get rid of him? As Gilles had said, a thief is only afraid of someone who can give him away. Was it because Vincent had come across him in the snowstorm? And, again, the night that Miski had been so brutally wounded?

All at once he was seized with a fantastic desire to climb down the rock face and confront Rapalli, demanding to know what he was up to. He was so anxious to find out, and to clear Alberto, that he felt ready for heroic deeds and dauntless daring. Rapalli's huge breadth showed that he was very strong, but on his side Vincent had the agility of his fourteen years. He would know how to defend himself all right, if he were attacked. He clenched his fists, and was just about to clamber down, when he halted abruptly. Even if he were able to overcome this man, he would gain nothing from it. Whatever happened, Rapalli would give nothing away, and every chance of getting him later would be lost.

"No, I mustn't."

Vincent just clenched his fists tighter as he went on looking at the shape crouched at the side of the path. Then, glancing toward the east, he became aware of a long whitish trail stretching over the Piedmont plain. Dawn was coming. He picked himself up, and went on his way.

The sun had already risen by the time he reached Young Deer Pass. His heart was heavy as he crossed the frontier, and he felt no relief at being safe again. He had escaped from the police: he had not fallen victim to Rapalli's treachery: but the money entrusted to him by Alberto had been taken from him. Rosalba and her mother could not leave, and once more, because of that money, they would be harassed by the police. He had so much wanted to help Alberto, and all he had done was to make it seem even more certain that he was guilty. Vincent had thought he was a man now, but he had behaved like a child.

In spite of the cold, which the warm rays of the sun had done nothing yet to disperse, he sat down on a rock.

"Just a kid, that's all I am," he said. "A kid."

And when you are fourteen and ready to change the face of the world, it is the worst disillusion of all to realize that you are still only a boy.

11

The Round Stone

ONCE back at Wolf Ridge, Vincent did not even wait to tell his friend what had happened to him.

"I'll tell you tomorrow, Gilles," was all that he said. "I must go down to Lauzière right away to see my parents."

Mounted on Bichounette, he set off immediately on the valley road, determined to tell them everything this time. He thought that everyone was staring at him when he came into the village, and he was very worried by the time he rode into the courtyard at the farm.

"Hallo!" was all that his father said, watching him jump off the mule. "You're back a day earlier than I expected. Did you run short of food?"

So he knew nothing. Once Vincent had escaped, the Italian police must have decided not to tell his parents or the French police. They were probably not at all sorry to avoid in this way all sorts of complications and useless paper work.

When he entered the house, however, he found his mother in a very worried state, but not because of him. For the last three days his little brother, who was delicate, had been running a temperature for which the local doctor could find no cause. She paid scarcely any attention to her big son Vincent, not even noticing that he was a day early.

The young mountain lad found his resolution faltering. Since it was all over and he had come back safe and sound, what was the point of worrying his mother, who had quite enough to worry about with his brother. He decided that once more he would hold his tongue; but since his conscience was bothering him, he made a secret vow that he would not go back to Argentera.

He returned to Wolf Ridge the following day. Gilles had wasted no time while he was away. He had cut the hay on the whole of a long slope, and had looked after Miski, whose wound was healing nicely, and who was beginning to run around the hut again on three legs.

That evening after supper, the two boys sat on the floor in front of the roaring stove and talked. Gilles was all eagerness to know what had happened to his friend. Vincent began the story of his adventures in great detail, and Gilles shivered as he listened. Though he had never met either Alberto or Rosalba, he now shared the friendship Vincent felt for them, and he too was anxious to free them from the terrible injustice that had made their lives a misery.

"I'm absolutely with you," Gilles said. "I'm as sure as you are now that Rapalli is the thief. But I still find it difficult to explain some of the things that have happened. Why did he want to make sure you disappeared? You were in the hands of the police, so he had nothing more to fear from you."

"He must have thought that he had, Gilles."

"He couldn't have been afraid that you'd give him away—you knew hardly anything. What could you have told the police? Only that you met a man you thought was Rapalli one night in a snowstorm, then again on the road to the pass, where he stabbed Miski with a knife. The only real evidence you have is the knotted rope—but all the ropes on the haycarts are the same, so how could you prove it was his? As for the button, Rapalli probably doesn't even know that he lost it up there, and he certainly doesn't know that you found it. You can't even be sure that he recognized you that night he attacked Miski. For, as you told me, you yourself only saw a shadow among the rocks."

"Gilles, I think you're wrong there. Rapalli could easily have recognized me: I was standing just where I would show up most against the dark sky. And that's why he started immediately to dodge among the rocks. Remember that I spoke to this Rapalli the first time I went to Argentera. And since I had no reason then to mistrust him, I told him a great deal. He knows that this hut on Wolf Ridge is the only one near the road to the pass."

Gilles thought hard, propping his fists under his chin and following his own line of reasoning.

"Go and fetch the knotted rope, Vincent, so that we can look it over more carefully."

Vincent brought it from the hayloft, where he had hidden it, and they examined it thoroughly from end to end, poring over it as though each knot concealed a secret. But they discovered nothing new. The iron hook at one end had obviously been made by hand, roughly beaten out with a hammer. It was clear, as Vincent had already supposed, that this strange apparatus must be needed for some difficult crossing, but where? And, most important of all, what had it to do with the disappearance of the gold cross?

They sighed as they coiled it up again, not knowing what to think, yet somehow sure that this rope would lead them to discover Rapalli's secret, if anything would.

By the time they went to bed that night, darkness had long since descended upon Wolf Ridge and enfolded the whole mountain range in an immense quiet. Just before he fell asleep, Vincent's thoughts returned to the little house with the red shutters. He still felt guilty when he thought of Rosalba, because he had given up the money that she and her mother needed so badly. He wondered what had happened since he left, and whether they had been accused of helping him to escape. Oh, why had that stupid frontier, so easy to cross the first time, now become an insurmountable barrier?

He woke the next morning with an aching head, but, with Gilles beside him, set to work in a sort of frenzy, more to forget his thoughts than to make up for lost time. By the end of the afternoon, he could hold out no longer.

"Gilles, I've just got to go up as far as the pass. I can't stop wondering whether Rosalba hasn't already been up there."

Gilles was surprised by this sudden decision.

"Now? Why not go tomorrow morning, after a good night's sleep?"

Vincent pointed to the mountain.

"Look at those little clouds capping the Malacosta and the peak of the Dard. The weather's going to change."

That was only a pretext, of course.

"Do you want me to come with you?" Gilles asked.

"I think one of us ought to stay in the hut; Miski would want to follow us and he's not well enough yet. . . . And then, Alberto might come up again; he said he would if he could."

Gilles dropped the subject, though he would

very much have liked to go with him. He just put his hand on Vincent's shoulder.

"Now, promise. If you don't find anything up there, don't go beyond the frontier; don't go back to Argentera."

Vincent smiled a little sadly.

"I promise, Gilles. I'll be back before midnight."

He set out on foot, without Bichounette, who had been working hard all day bringing in the hay piled up on the slopes; and, of course, without Miski. The weather was fine in the west, but on the peaks the cloud caps were growing thicker, and beginning to merge with each other.

Vincent went along at a good swinging pace, quite certain that a message awaited him up there. Somehow he was already dreading that message, as though only bad news could be expected.

He had just left the grassy slopes at the end of Wolf Ridge behind him and was about to set out on the road to the pass when all at once the sound of rapid panting behind him made him turn around.

"Oh, Miski!"

The faithful dog had not been able to resist temptation any more than his master had. Though he had looked up with a grieved air at Vincent as he left the hut, he had given no sign that he intended escaping from Gilles's watchfulness. He had bounded off at the first

opportunity, though, and had arrived on three feet, panting hard. Vincent scolded him thoroughly, and would have liked to send him back, but the hut was already a considerable distance away. Instead of going back, Miski would simply pretend to set off, and then hide until his master returned.

"All right, then," Vincent said. "I'd better take you along."

He scolded the dog again as if he were a naughty child, to make his displeasure absolutely clear, and then they set off together, Miski following behind, as a sign of submissiveness. The air had grown noticeably still, not with the heavy calm that presages a storm, but with that sort of stillness that brings mist in its train. The thought did not worry Vincent unduly, for he was wearing his raincoat, and he knew the way so well by now that he could not get lost.

As dusk came upon them, the boy and the dog were climbing steadily. All at once Miski stopped, and then began to sniff the ground with great eagerness. Vincent, very annoyed, called him to order.

"Now then, Miski, don't start that again! You ought to know by now what it costs to run after shadows."

However, since Rapalli was much on his mind, Vincent went back to the dog to see what had excited him. This time it was not a sound, but some sort of smell on the path that had roused Miski's interest—the scent of an animal probably, for at that point there were tracks branching off to lose themselves on the mountainside.

"Oh, come on, Miski, we've no time to lose if we're to get there before nightfall!"

They set off again, but soon found themselves plunging into a mist like cottonwool, that stayed with them all the way up to the summit of the pass.

His heart beating fast, Vincent rushed to the post, and counted three paces, medium paces, since Rosalba was smaller than he. At once he caught sight of a flat round stone. It was rather larger than the others, and it was quite clear to anyone on the look-out that it had been placed there deliberately. He bent down and picked it up . . . there was nothing underneath. He could only think that he had, after all, made a mistake and one by one he turned over all the other stones in that area. Nothing. Puzzled, he began to wonder whether Rosalba had come. He was just going to search the other side of the post, in case she had mistaken the direction, when Miski, who had gone off on his own, appeared before him all at once, holding something in his mouth like a trophy.

"The case!"

Vincent snatched it from the dog. The spectacle case was open, the lid wobbling on its hinge. And there was nothing inside it. With feverish haste Vincent tore the cloth lining open, in case Rosalba had wanted to hide her message more thoroughly. There was nothing there either. He questioned Miski who, seeing that his master was interested in his find, began wagging his tail.

"Where did you find this? Show me! Show me!"

The animal seemed to understand. Vincent handed back the case, and the dog seized it in his jaws and put it down several feet away, where he had found it. But there also Vincent found nothing. Even in this fading light, he would have been able to see the white paper of Rosalba's note if it were lying anywhere about. So Miski could not have dropped it when he got hold of the case.

Vincent didn't know what to think. Perhaps the wind had carried the case away. . . . But why was it open? And why hadn't Rosalba hidden it under that stone near the post? Perhaps she had, and someone had found the case, and thrown it away after taking the message it held. That seemed to be the only explanation. But passers-by were rare on that path, and who would have thought of lifting that special stone, when it was well away from the path? Could it have been done by chance?

Downcast, Vincent turned the case over in his fingers, finding no answer to these questions. One thing was certain: Rosalba had been there, and her secret had been betrayed. Something terrible must have happened to her, and he did not know how to find out what it was.

Instinctively he turned toward Piedmont as though to question the valley itself, hidden from him by the mist. Suddenly he felt an overwhelming desire to go to Argentera.

"No," a still, small voice seemed to say within him. "Think of your promise, and don't act stupidly again. You know that you must go back to Wolf Ridge."

The still, small voice was insistent, but there was another that made itself felt, the voice of his indignation and of his friendship for the Italian girl.

Yet he knew that he must not go. At last he took from his pocket a small notebook that he had brought with him, and tore a sheet from it. He placed the paper on a stone and wrote with a hand shaking with cold and distress:

"Rosalba, I came . . . I found only the empty case, thrown a long way from the stone. I don't understand. I'm so afraid that something may have happened to you. If you get this note, tell me what happened. I'll come tomorrow and every day if necessary.

                                        Vincent."

He folded the sheet of paper, which was not easy to read since his writing was unsteady and betrayed how upset he was. He put it into the case, and placed it under the round stone. Even as he did so, he felt that it was useless . . . Rosalba would not come again.

12

Traces of Blood

ONE last look toward Italy, and Vincent set out on his journey back to Wolf Ridge. In the meantime, darkness had spread over the mountains, a dank, sticky, thick, and sinister dark. Miski seemed to sense his master's sadness. He padded along with his head down, occasionally shaking his thick coat to get rid of the fine drops of moisture that clung to it.

Vincent took the downward path very reluctantly. Once or twice he stopped, on the verge of going back to the top again. But he knew that it would simply be asking for trouble to go back to Argentera. He could not do it; he had promised. Nothing, however, could prevent his thoughts from concentrating upon Rosalba. Where was she? . . . What had happened to her?

He had been walking more than an hour when Miski stopped again abruptly in the middle of the path, growling quietly to himself in a meaningful sort of way.

"Now then, Miski, what's the matter?"

Vincent saw that they had come to the place where the dog had stopped on the way up. Struck by the animal's obstinacy, he went and stood beside him, but the night was too dark, and he could see nothing. Miski refused to budge, so Vincent took out a box of matches he had brought with him in place of the flashlight the police had taken from him in Argentera. He bent over the path in the fragile light that pierced the darkness. Blood. He pushed Miski aside and squatted down to see better. Yes, it really was blood, just a spot not much bigger than a coin, but still red, not yet dry. It didn't necessarily mean very much. This place was a sort of crossroads that must be frequented by all sorts of mountain beasts. Maybe an eagle or some other bird of prey had devoured its victim there. Even so, Vincent was disturbed.

While he was thinking things over, Miski, delighted that his master was taking an interest in his discovery, had moved a few feet away in search of other succulent smells, and now he began to growl again. Vincent went over to him, and saw another spot of blood . . . and another, smaller now, but always on the same path, the one leading away from Wolf Ridge. A third match had just gone out when Vincent noticed that Miski had scented, not more blood, but something that looked like a worm, or a little snake. It was a shoelace. He lit another match and saw that it was not a whole cord, but only a piece of one. There was a sort of small pompon on one end, so it was not from a man's shoe. He thought at once of Rosalba. The first time he went to Argentera, Rosalba had been wearing shoes with white laces . . . like this one!

His heart began to beat faster. Could Rosalba have come as far as this? Had she injured herself on the mountainside? Anxiously he called Miski, who had run on ahead.

"Stay by me, Miski, don't leave my side. We're going to follow this trail."

He set out along the path, which was quite unknown to him. The mist was not as thick as it had been near the pass, but the night was very dark. As he walked along, Vincent tried to work it out. If Rosalba had come far enough to get lost on this slope, why had she left a message near the pass? And still more important, why had the case no longer been under the stone?

In front of him, Miski was scenting every rock. The traces of blood had stopped, but the dog's persistence left no doubt that someone had passed that way not long before. Vincent began calling:

"Rosalba!"

Only the echo answered him. There was hardly any path at all, and from time to time he lost his way completely on the bare slopes; but Miski, for his part, went straight on without a moment's pause.

They had been walking for more than an hour and Vincent, after several calls that had brought no response, was just beginning to wonder where his dog was leading him. Then all at once the animal stopped dead, his neck stretched and his ears pricked. Vincent stopped too, listened and called again. Nothing. Yet Miski had certainly seen something; he knew his dog well enough for that. Another match flamed, and Vincent cried out:

"Rosalba!"

He rushed up to her. She was lying about five feet away, in a rocky hollow, quite still, with her head hanging limply as though she were dead. Blood was running from her right leg, above the knee. He caught up her hand; it was warm. Her heart was still beating—not very strongly, but it was beating. He attempted to lift her head. A faint groan escaped her lips,

but her eyes did not open. Vincent dropped to his knees beside her limp body and called to her softly.

"Rosalba . . . it's Vincent . . . your friend Vincent."

The girl heard nothing. Vincent lit another match, to look at the injury. It did not seem to be deep, in spite of all the blood, and he was sure her leg was not broken. She must have been hurt near the place where Miski had found the first traces of blood, and she could not have made her way so far afterward with a broken leg. He cleansed the wound with his handkerchief. He wondered how long Rosalba had been lying there unconscious in the cold night. How could he save her? . . . By carrying her to the hut? But the hut was a long way away. By night, and without a light, it would take him several hours, even if he were lucky enough not to stumble and fall with her on this rough and unfamiliar path. It was impossible; and yet she could not stay where she was, in the increasing cold. He took off his raincoat, and then his jacket, and carefully wrapped them around her.

It was then that he thought of his dog, who was gently licking Rosalba's hand, as though to help his master in keeping her warm.

Miski was intelligent, stubborn like all young dogs, but capable of great understanding. Vincent tore a sheet from his notebook. Holding a match in one hand and his pencil in the other, he scribbled:

"Help! Rosalba unconscious on the mountainside. Come with Bichounette. Miski will guide you. Come quickly."

He folded the paper and tore off a piece of his handkerchief, being careful to choose a part that was not bloodstained, so that Gilles would not be too worried. With this strip he fixed the message to Miski's collar.

"Go, Miski! Back to the hut, quick! D'you understand, to the hut!"

The animal looked at his master with alert eyes shining in the darkness. He knew that this time his master was asking him for help, not chasing him away, and after one last caress he shot off into the night, with little regard for the shoulder that still hurt him.

Alone with Rosalba, Vincent fell prey to another terrible anxiety. Suppose Miski did not lead Gilles to them? Suppose Rosalba died of exposure before his very eyes? It was only just midnight, four long hours until dawn; and the hours before dawn on the mountainside are always icy.

He touched her still hands again, and it seemed to him that they were growing cold. He began to rub her limbs, trying to rouse her.

"Rosalba, wake up!"

At last, the girl quivered, and then began to shiver all over. Her eyes half opened.

"Rosalba, it's your friend Vincent . . . Do speak to me!"

She did not answer. She was still only semi-conscious.

"Where am I?" she murmured. "Who brought me here?"

"Don't you recognize the voice of your friend Vincent?"

In the thick darkness, she could not make out the features of the face bent over her. Vincent struck a match, the last. Blinded, Rosalba shut her eyes, then opened them again, and at last she recognized him.

"Oh, it's you! Am I on Wolf Ridge?"

"Not yet, unfortunately, Rosalba."

"Where am I, then?"

She was not yet aware of what had happened to her; then suddenly she shuddered.

"And the man?"

"What man?"

"The one who followed me."

"I don't know what you mean, Rosalba."

She passed a hand over her forehead.

"Oh, do try to tell me, Rosalba! This evening I went up to Young Deer Pass and found the spectacle case you were going to put your letter in. But it was empty, and you hadn't hidden it. What happened?"

Rosalba was still hovering on the edge of unconsciousness, and he had to repeat the question several times.

"Yes, the case!" she murmured at last.

She fell silent, making great efforts to remember. Then, utterly overwrought, she burst

147

into tears. Vincent did not know how to help her.

"It's all too awful," she sobbed, ". . . the police . . . the man. . . ."

"Tell me, Rosalba."

"This morning when they found out that you'd escaped, the police came to our house again. They accused us of having helped you. They took my mother away to prison, in Sallega. I wanted to go too, to be shut up with her, but they wouldn't let me because I'm too young. They took me to a great-aunt who lives in the village and told her to look after me."

"Did you climb up to the pass to tell me this?"

"Yes, Vincent, to ask if you could help us . . . my mother . . ."

"What happened up there?"

"I left my great-aunt's house just after midday, while the village was deserted. I was so afraid someone might guess where I was going. No one saw me. But I didn't know the pass was so high up. I went on walking and walking, and I thought I would never get there. The mist came down, but I still went on to the very end. Then I looked for a big stone to put the case under, and carried it to the frontier post and three paces off, as you had said. Just as I was going to put the note in the case and slip it under the stone, I heard the sounds of footsteps on the path, coming from the Italian side. I was so terrified I just ran away on the other side."

"But the case, Rosalba? You did have time to hide it?"

She did not answer at once, trying to remember, and then she shook her head.

"No, I didn't have time. Oh yes, I remember now. As I was running away I heard something fall from my pocket—I suppose it was the case . . . I must have the letter still with me."

She slid her hand into the pocket of her dress, and drew from it a crumpled piece of paper that Vincent could not attempt to read, since he had used his last match.

"And then, Rosalba?"

"I ran for ages. I thought I was being followed. When I couldn't run anymore, I stood by the side of the path, and I was still terrified. Then I thought of Wolf Ridge, and I started walking again to get to you."

Worn out with so much talking she stopped, and her head fell onto Vincent's shoulder. After a minute or two, breathlessly, and in a whisper, she went on:

"Then I fell, and hurt myself badly. My leg began to bleed, and I was afraid I wouldn't be able to get up again. But I did set off again . . . and then all at once, I don't know what happened, everything looked blurred, the mountains and the rocks began to whirl around, and I felt as though the ground were giving way beneath my feet . . . After that I knew nothing more."

She stopped speaking, and began crying softly. With a sudden start, she took hold of Vincent's hands.

"I don't want to go back to Argentera now that they've taken my mother away. Let me stay with you; take me to your hut."

She was shaking so much that Vincent didn't know what to do.

"Are you still cold, or in pain?"

She let herself be wrapped in the raincoat as if she were a little child, and for a long time leaned against Vincent, who could not stop thinking about the fright she had had up on the pass.

"Rosalba, you're quite sure you heard footsteps when you were terrified up there on the pass?"

"Oh yes, someone was climbing up behind me."

"And you didn't see anything?"

"It was misty . . . and I ran away as quickly as I could."

"Did you get the impression that you'd been seen . . . that someone was after you?"

She shook her head slowly.

"No, I don't know . . . I didn't hear anything anymore . . . nor see anything, except for a light, just before I fell here. I remember that I thought it was the light from your hut, except that it seemed to move, like a lantern being carried."

Poor Rosalba! It seemed obvious that she had already been on the verge of unconsciousness, and had seen everything spinning around.

"No, Rosalba, it wasn't the light on Wolf Ridge—you can't see it from here. . . . From what side did you see it gleaming?"

"I don't know anymore, it was already very dark. Over there perhaps—yes, over there."

She pointed in the direction where the mountain descended almost vertically to the Black Abyss, whose barren slopes had never sheltered a single hut. Her arm dropped, as though even that slight effort had exhausted her. Her head came to rest on Vincent's shoulder, and she slept.

"A light," Vincent murmured to himself. "A light that moved."

He said no more, and the immense silence of the mountains enfolded them.

13

The Black Abyss

NIGHT was nearly spent when Miski, running ahead of Bichounette, loomed out of the darkness and dropped, panting, at his master's feet. Exhausted, the brave dog had accomplished his mission. A few moments later Gilles arrived, and dismounted with his lantern. When he saw Rosalba lying motionless, her eyes closed, he thought he had come too late.

"Oh, is she . . . ?"

"No, Gilles, she's fallen asleep. She's completely worn out."

Vincent's friend eased off the straps of his rucksack and took from it a bottle of fresh water. Next he dragged from Bichounette's back the blanket he had also thought of bringing. Vincent bathed Rosalba's face with some of the water, and cleaned the wound again. It was no longer bleeding.

"How pale she is!" whispered Gilles, who was directing the light of the lantern toward Vincent. "How are we going to get her back?"

"You can help me to settle her on Bichounette; then I'll jump up behind to keep her from falling off."

Vincent nudged her gently and she groaned as she opened her eyes. When she caught sight of a strange face in the light of the lantern, she uttered a cry of terror.

"There's nothing to be afraid of, Rosalba. This is my friend Gilles. . . . He's your friend, too. He came with the mule to bring you back to the hut on Wolf Ridge."

Reassured, she tried to sit up, while Vincent made her swallow a few drops of water. She wanted to get up without help, but she was only just on her feet when she swayed, her knees buckling under her. She would have fallen if Vincent and Gilles between them had not hoisted her up onto the back of the mule. They settled her as comfortably as they could and wrapped the blanket around her shoulders. Then, shivering with cold, Vincent put on his jacket and his raincoat, and jumped up behind her.

The little band set off, led by Miski, who was now so tired that his leg was hurting him again, and he trotted along on three only. Gilles walked in front of the mule, lighting the way with the lantern. Rosalba, only half-conscious, let herself be carried along, and Vincent, who was holding her up in his strong arms, saw that she had soon fallen asleep again. He could not stop thinking about what had happened to her, and her terror on Young Deer Pass. It was difficult to know whether someone had really followed her up to the pass. Who could it be who was ready to cross the frontier? Still more important, how was it that the footsteps had not caught up with her when she had stayed so long at the side of the path? Rapalli, if it were he, must have gone off in another direction: and if so, which? And for what purpose?

They had been walking for a good half hour, and would soon be reaching the mule track, when Gilles, who was still ahead, came to a halt.

"What is it?" asked Vincent.

Gilles came to a stand beside the mule, and pointed with his arm outstretched.

"Over there—look!"

"Where? I can't see anything."

"That little speck of light, at the bottom of the mountain, there where the dark is so thick."

Vincent stared in the direction indicated by his friend, and then he saw it. It was a microscopic gleam, like the pricking of a star, which came and went and seemed to be moving.

"What is it?" exclaimed Rosalba, roused from sleep by the sudden halt and the broken silence. "Are we in danger?"

She looked in the direction Gilles was pointing out.

"Oh, the light . . . the light that moves . . . That's the one. I recognize it."

Almost at once the light went out and did not reappear. There was no possible doubt as far as Vincent was concerned, for he knew this part of the mountain better than Gilles. The light had come from the Black Abyss.

In a voice choked with excitement Vincent said:

"That light! The Black Abyss . . . The rope!"

The light—the Black Abyss—the rope. Gilles understood now, too, and wondered why neither of them had been able to put things together before. It was so clear now that that odd rope was needed for climbing into a ravine. The light that appeared and disappeared belonged to a man who was either preparing to go down the abyss, or had just climbed out of it. . . . Who could he be? Rapalli!

Unfortunately, it was out of the question just now to brave the danger of darkness, and climb down there to investigate. Rosalba was cold and in pain, and her life was more precious than anything else.

"Quick, Gilles, let's get going!"

For the rest of the way, the two friends did not exchange a single word, and Rosalba dropped off to sleep again. At last they came to Wolf Ridge. While Gilles hastened to relight the stove with a huge armful of hay that roared like the furnace of a smithy, Vincent looked after Rosalba, preparing a bunk for her where she could stretch out comfortably under two warm

blankets. He made her drink a cup of scalding coffee. In the warmth and quiet of the hut she stopped shivering at last, and color came back into her cheeks.

"Rosalba, how do you feel? Are you still in pain?"

"No, not any more. And I'm not scared any more. I feel fine."

She smiled in relief, looking first at Gilles and

then at Vincent as if to thank them, after which, utterly at peace, she fell asleep again.

The two friends were silent, standing before the bunk in which she rested so tranquilly, watching her sleep. But both of them were disturbed.

Vincent said abruptly, keeping his voice low:

"Gilles, she's safe now, she doesn't need us both to watch over her. I must go back there and find out what it's all about."

"Oh Vincent, not to the Black Abyss while it's still dark!"

"It's our biggest chance! In a little while it may be too late. It will soon be dawn now, anyway."

"Vincent, you can't go; you're too tired. Let me go, and you stay with Rosalba."

Vincent hesitated. He was tired and he had been frozen through while he sat beside Rosalba. But was Gilles able to take his place?

"No, Gilles, I don't think so. I know the way; last year I climbed down once to the very edge of the abyss. Besides, you don't know Rapalli. Oh, Gilles, if only it's him, and we can prove that he stole the gold cross of Santa Anna!"

His voice broke with excitement. He took Gilles's rucksack, put the knotted rope in it, on the off-chance that he might need it, and lit the lantern again. He leaned over to take one last look at Rosalba, whose breathing was regular, and who was peacefully sleeping; and then he clasped his friend's hand tightly.

"Gilles, we really are going to clear Alberto's name!"

Outside, the pallid gleam of greenish light stretching behind the high peaks did nothing to dispel the darkness, but the last traces of mist had gone. Vincent went quickly along Wolf Ridge and arrived at the great rock wall that descended in a dizzy slope to the lip of the Black Abyss. He halted there, and peered into the pitch-black depths. The light had gone, and he wondered if he had come too late.

With infinite care he set out on the perilous descent. He hooked the lantern on his belt to keep his hands free, and slowly drew near the abyss, clinging to the jagged points as they loomed out of the darkness in the early dawn light. He was only about nine hundred feet away, as the crow flies, but the smooth wall, offering no foothold, forced him all the time to travel in whatever direction seemed possible. At last he came to the immediate surroundings of the abyss, a fantastic huddle of great rocks. Among them gaped an immense hole, from which came the distant muted sound of subterranean waters.

He listened for a long while before he approached the edge, trying to sense the presence of any other person. When finally he rounded the huddle of great rocks, he halted abruptly. There, almost at his feet, he saw a rope looped around the sharp point of a rock.

"A rope! Like the one Rapalli lost!"

Had any doubt remained in his mind, it ended there once and for all. He crept carefully forward, and leaned over into space, trying to see where the knotted rope ended. Unfortunately, he could only see as far as the third knot: the rest of the rope was lost in the inky depths. He leaned over still further, and listened again. There was no sound rising above the rushing of the distant waters. He ventured to touch the rope, which stirred gently. There was nothing hanging from the other end, then, nor did it seem to be fixed to anything down there. He drew it carefully up to him, and it came without resistance, with a slight sound of rubbing against the rock. It was longer than the other, a good forty-five feet, with eighteen knots.

Vincent thought quickly. If that rope belonged to Rapalli, as he grew increasingly convinced that it did, what was it doing there? Had Rapalli left it when he climbed out of the hole? . . . Or was he still somewhere down in those depths? At least three hours had gone by since that moment when the light had appeared for the last time, as they were taking Rosalba back to the hut.

Three hours! That was a very long time. The man had probably climbed up again, as day was approaching, and set out over the mountain, leaving behind the rope he was sure no one would discover. It seemed, then, that he intended to come back some other night, though Vincent could not imagine for what reason.

He wondered what was at the bottom of the abyss, and what Rapalli had come to seek or to see. Was there any connection with the theft of the gold cross? Leaning over the gaping hole, Vincent looked down into space and wondered: but no inspiration came out of those depths. Very slowly and carefully, he let the rope down again to the very last knot, so that it did not look as though any hand had touched it.

"It's a question of waiting and watching," he said to himself. "I'll come again tomorrow night and every other night, and hide here, and in the end I'll find out what's going on."

Now the whole mountainside was flooded with daylight. He thought of Rosalba, who might already be awake. He wondered what was best for her until matters were cleared up. She could not stay in the hut; he would have to take her home to Lauzière. Of course, that meant that he would have to tell his parents everything, and he knew that it would be a great relief to him to do so. He knew, too, that his mother would be only too glad to take care of her.

It was time to set out on his return journey but something stronger than he would not let him leave that black opening. He was drawn to that rope as though the key to the mystery were attached to its other end, and he desperately wanted to go and see if that were so.

He knew that he was afraid all right, deeply afraid. He had heard, as a child, so many sinister stories told about this Black Abyss. . . . But he was no longer a child, and he was well developed for his age. One of his chief amusements last winter at Lauzière had been climbing down the hay ropes he had slung from the rafters in the barn. He decided to climb down by the knots, and find out for himself whether the rope reached the bottom of the abyss . . . and then perhaps he would understand why Rapalli had come here.

He looked at the rope for a long time. He handled it again, and made sure that the loop around the jutting rock was in no danger of coming undone. Then he relit his lantern and hooked it onto his belt again, to one side, so that it would not get in his way. Hanging on to the rope with all his strength and all his courage, he let himself down into space.

14
Rope's End

KNOT by knot he let himself glide slowly down into the darkness, his head turned toward his shoulder in an attempt to fathom the depths of the abyss. But the dim light of the candle in his lantern served only to pick out the wall of rock against which the rope was hanging. He counted the knots so as to check the distance he had covered. When it came to the tenth, he stayed still, with a feeling that he was already far below the earth's surface. Yet below him the same thick darkness reigned, and he was seized with a terrible panic. To be quite certain that he would have enough strength to get to the surface again, when the time came, he climbed up a knot, and then another. He found that his muscles were strong, and reassured, he set out on his long descent again. His feet were gripping the twelfth, and then the thirteenth knot, when he saw a rock ledge glimmering faintly beneath him. Was this the bottom of the abyss? Two more knots, and his feet touched the ground.

For a few moments he stood still, listening hard. Next he detached his lantern from his belt with very great care, and held it at arm's length, sending the pallid light around him without moving from his position. Afterward he lowered it to ground level. The rock on which he stood formed a sort of shelf about three feet wide. Beneath, another abyss opened up, and from its depths the sound of rushing waters could be heard more distinctly.

Vincent ventured carefully along this wet and slippery ledge. He soon found himself in a sort of cave that was probably vast, since its wall remained hidden in shadow in spite of the light from the lantern. He wondered whether Rapalli had simply wished to explore this grotto—or what he had expected to find in it.

The ledge continued before him, running around the second abyss, and widening in the end to form a rock chamber about as big as the hayloft of the hut. Beyond this the ledge grew narrow again, and, as he walked along it, Vincent had the impression that he was coming back, from the other side of the abyss, to the place where his feet had first touched the ground. When he raised his head, he did see, almost immediately above him, the hole by which he had climbed down. But it was impossible to complete the tour of the grotto: the ledge narrowed so much that it became absolutely impassable.

Much disappointed, Vincent was about to turn back when he saw at his feet, as he lowered his lantern, another rope, also fastened to a jutting rock, but this time by means of an iron hook exactly like the one on the rope that Rapalli had left behind on Young Deer Pass. As he knelt down to examine it more closely, he held his lantern out to see how far the rope went down, and finally he took hold of it. Like the other, it had great knots in it and was hanging free. He pulled it up counting the knots, and found that there were twenty-one of them.

Once more he hesitated, gripped by terror: terror of the unknown, and of darkness. Yet feeling that he was drawing near his goal, he set out on the new descent. This time it was slow, careful, and very frightening, for the whole length of the rope was dripping with moisture. At every knot he stopped, held his breath, and listened. Above him, he could no longer see the point of light that had been so comforting only a little while ago, and he was afraid that his lantern might go out by accident.

He stopped at the tenth knot, breathless, wondering whether he had enough courage to continue. Come on, Vincent, you're grown-up now, show a bit of spunk!

Suddenly he started. He had heard another sound mingling with the dull murmur of the water running below, the sound of groaning. His fingers clenched round the rope, he came to an abrupt halt, and listened closely. He waited a while, but he did not hear the groaning again.

So he went on sliding down the rope; one knot . . . two . . . three knots slipped beneath his fingers, which were stiffened with the strain put upon them. Once more he came to a sudden halt. This time it was not a groaning or moaning that he heard, but a cry for help. He shook so much that the rope vibrated from top to bottom, and he had to clutch harder so that he would not fall. He hung like that above empty space, trying to pierce the darkness.

The lantern hooked to his belt lit only the rock wall backing his descent. He got hold of the lantern and tried to move it so as to see further into the depths. But he had overrated his strength. Just as he unhooked it, he felt his other hand slipping. Instinctively, he seized hold of the rope, dropping the lantern which knocked against a rock, rebounded onto another, broke in pieces, and fell into the subterranean river, leaving Vincent in total darkness.

It all happened so quickly that he did not at first realize what had taken place. Hanging by his arms, already exhausted, he grew panic-stricken, and his strength gave out. It seemed impossible to climb up. All he could do was slide down to the end of the rope. When at last his feet touched the bottom of the abyss, he found that he could hardly stand. He stayed there a long time, shivering and on the verge of losing consciousness. Where was the man who had called out to him? He had a strong feeling that man was Rapalli.

A cold sweat beaded his brow. Somewhere near him was a man, ill or wounded and in danger, who had called to him: yet now he could hear nothing at all.

Gathering up all his courage, he called out. His voice resounded mournfully as though it were echoing through a cave, but no other voice, no sound of groaning, answered him.

Vincent did not know what to do. How could he try to reach the man, with nothing to guide him in this absolute darkness? He would only risk drowning in the river that he sensed was quite near, even though he could not see it.

He was still grasping the end of the dank rope, for fear of losing it.

"I'll have to climb up again, and get back quickly to the hut so that Gilles can go down into the valley and fetch help."

But he had no more strength. He was so cold and so afraid, worn out by all he had gone through. His body had become a dead weight, and every attempt to climb up a knot left him breathless, for his feet could no longer get a grip on the rope.

After much struggling he did manage to inch his way up the rope, only to be defeated by the still more violent effort that was required to hoist himself onto the slippery ledge. After two un-

successful attempts he gave a mighty heave and threw himself flat on his stomach onto a jutting rock, while his feet, desperately threshing about in space, at last found a foothold. He collapsed on the ledge, fighting for breath, and utterly spent. He lay stretched out on the wet stone for a long time, waiting for the thudding of his heart to calm down. Then he stood up on the slippery ledge, and began to feel his way around the grotto. He stopped several times, thinking that he heard muffled groans coming from the depths of the lower abyss, but it was only the sound of the water.

At last he reached the place beneath the point of light, and his courage came back to him. The long rope was still waiting there for him. He filled his lungs with air to renew his strength, and started out on the second climb, his face lifted to the daylight as though it helped him. The hole gradually grew larger. The rope, his hands, the rock wall emerged from the darkness, and there were only four more knots to go. One last pull, and he found himself on the surface, completely blinded by the midday sun.

He himself was safe and sound, but a man was lying in danger at the bottom of the abyss. Even if it were Rapalli, he must still be saved . . . then maybe his secret would be revealed at last. Without waiting for the erratic thudding of his heart to die down, he clambered over the maze of rocks. His legs were heavy as lead, and from time to time everything was blotted from sight, making him wonder if he were going to lose consciousness, like Rosalba. Each step cost him a considerable effort. He had to sit down and wait a while. Everything was going round . . . Where had he come from? . . . Where was he going to? . . . Ah yes, Wolf Ridge . . . the hut . . . Rosalba. How far away it all seemed, and how confused.

He wanted to get up and go on, but he hadn't the strength. All at once he lifted his head, for he thought that someone had called him. Was he still at the bottom of the abyss, then?

"Vincent, I've been looking everywhere for you! But what on earth's happened? Your hands are skinned raw, and your face is covered with mud."

That wasn't Rapalli's voice. It was his friend Gilles.

"Vincent, are you hurt?"

He looked at his hands and was surprised to see them covered with blood.

"It's nothing, Gilles. Help me . . . quick . . . the abyss . . . Rapalli."

He began to walk up the steep slope, supported by his friend. Gilles tried to find out what had happened, but Vincent, still in a daze, could only reply with little broken phrases:

"Black Abyss . . . Rapalli . . . the gold cross."

It was past noon when at last they reached the hut. Rosalba, fully restored by her long sleep, uttered a cry of distress when she saw Vincent come in, his face haggard and covered with mud. Then he collapsed full length on his bunk.

"Gilles, get Bichounette and go down at once to Lauzière. . . . Tell my father everything . . . then go to the police . . . the doctor . . . Tell them a man is dying at the bottom of the Black Abyss . . . Tell them to bring ropes and lanterns . . . Go quickly, Gilles."

He stopped speaking, drew a deep breath, then turned toward the girl.

"Rosalba . . . the gold cross . . . Rapalli . . . Oh, if only at last. . . ."

He did not finish what he had wanted to say. Overcome by exhaustion, he dropped off into a deep sleep.

170

15

The Third Abyss

WHEN Vincent woke up, he saw Rosalba's face leaning over him. Sitting up in the bunk, he asked her anxiously what time of day it was, and where his friend was.

"Gilles? . . . not here yet?

"He said it will take five or six hours before he's back. He hasn't been gone five yet."

Vincent swept a hand across his forehead.

"Not here yet! He'll be too late . . . too late."

His eyes darkened with sadness. Abruptly he threw back the cover that Rosalba had spread over him, and got to his feet.

"Too late!" he repeated. "I should have . . ."

He crossed the room, still reeling with exhaustion, and took down his jacket, which Rosalba had cleaned while he slept.

"Where are you going?"

He did not answer. She went up to him and took him by the arm, afraid that he was still in a sort of delirium.

"Where are you going, Vincent?"

"To the Black Abyss. I must."

"Oh, Vincent, you can hardly stand. Gilles will be back in less than an hour. You aren't fit enough to go."

Her voice was so gentle, and so persuasive, and he did indeed still feel so exhausted that he gave in, and went and sat on the edge of his bunk.

"You're right, Rosalba, I couldn't make it . . . and yet . . ."

He sighed deeply and turned his head away. "Rosalba," he said, "I'm absolutely convinced that it was Rapalli I heard at the bottom of the abyss. Perhaps I could have saved him. But it's too late now; he must be dead. We'll never know now."

He put his head in his hands, and began to cry like a child. Rosalba realized that he was suffering from reaction after all he had done. She remembered that he had spent most of the night watching beside her on the mountain, and that he had had practically nothing to eat for a long time. She tried to persuade him to have something. He shook his head, but when she insisted, he took a biscuit and a glass of water to drink with it. That was enough to give him a severe pain in his stomach, as the pangs of hunger suddenly gripped him. He cut himself a slice of bread and a piece of cheese and devoured them in four mouthfuls. . . . Then another . . . and a third. As the food disappeared, he felt as though fresh blood were surging in his veins, flooding him with renewed energy, and helping him to throw off his exhaustion.

He was just finishing his fourth slice when he pricked up his ears.

"Listen! They're here!"

They were, indeed; Gilles, with two policemen and the young doctor from Lauzière, a well-built, sporting type who regularly each winter beat all the boys of the region in the ski races.

"Your father didn't come up because of his back," Gilles explained quickly. "But he knows all about it. . . . We've got lamps and ropes. We'll be off at once."

"Me, too. I was waiting for you."

"Oh no!" Gilles protested. "You . . ."

"I've slept and I've eaten, and I'm all right again. Anyway, you need me to guide you: we'll lose less time if I do."

"Who will stay with Rosalba?"

"No one," the girl said quickly. "Just leave Miski with me. He knows me now, and I won't be afraid if he's here."

Vincent turned to her, and smiled his gratitude that she was willing to stay all alone in this isolated hut.

"Oh, Rosalba, just imagine if, when we come back . . ."

He stopped there, but she knew what he meant.

The little band set off at once. During the long climb, Gilles told Vincent what a hard time he'd had convincing the police, once he'd reached Lauzière. They had shaken their heads unbelievingly, but he had been so persistent that in the end they had come with him, grumbling all the time, convinced that they were being dragged into a useless expedition.

The sun was already low on the horizon when they reached the rim of the Black Abyss. The rope was still in its place, looped round the spur of rock and swinging in space. The older of the two policemen looked aghast at the gaping hole before him.

"You mean we're going down there on that rope?"

"You can wait here for us," his colleague said. "We'd better have someone stay up here, for anything might happen."

They switched on the electric lamps which each one of them had fixed to his belt. As an extra precaution the doctor had brought a lantern holding a candle, similar to the one Vincent had dropped, to test for any possible carbon monoxide in the atmosphere. In their knapsacks were extra ropes, in case they ran into trouble down below.

"Let me go first," said Vincent. "I'll call up as soon as I touch bottom. But go carefully—just about the eighth knot the rope rubs against a sharp rock."

He disappeared into the dark hole, slowly and carefully, and realized that he had got his second wind. He reached the first ledge without any difficulty. Then, one by one, Gilles, the doctor, and finally the policeman, came down to join him. The light from the lamps, so much stronger than the feeble flicker from his lantern, swept over the walls of the grotto, and showed Vincent that it was much bigger than he had imagined. All four held their breath and listened. Only the sound of rushing water came from below. They called three times, at intervals, but there was no reply.

In Indian file, with Vincent still in the lead, the four explorers crawled round the slippery ledge to reach the place where the second rope was fixed. Vincent found it without any trouble, just where he had left it.

It's longer than the other," he explained. "And that's when I dropped my lantern . . . But I did go down to the bottom all the same."

Flat on his stomach on the cold stone, the policeman leaned out, and tried to see to the bottom with his lamp.

"It's not possible," he said. "Just not possible. What on earth would a man be doing down there?"

But Vincent had already seized the rope and begun the next descent. This time he was not afraid; and he put out of his mind the fact that if the man who had called for help was Rapalli, he was the very one who had planned to hurl him into space. Only one thing mattered now, and that was to rescue the man.

Twice as he was climbing down he stopped to listen, but he heard nothing. The very second his feet touched solid rock, he unhooked his lamp and flashed it all around. He found himself once more on a rocky ledge. Below him, the abyss continued, pitch-black. There was no sign that any man had gone that way. When the other three had joined him, they all looked at each other, puzzled.

"You're quite sure you heard cries for help?" the policeman asked once more.

"Groaning, and then a cry. Yes, I'm absolutely certain."

It was Gilles, flat on his stomach, who slid forward first to the very edge, followed by Vincent, the doctor, and the policeman, who was grumbling all the time and saying that there was no point to it all.

Then Gilles came to a sudden halt.

"Look! . . . There's another rope!"

A third rope, fixed to the edge by an iron hook, hung in the third abyss. Vincent weighed this in his hand; it seemed lighter than the others. He brought it up slowly, and found that it ended at the eighth knot. They all leaned over to look at it closely, and saw that the rope had frayed and broken off. It was almost certain then that whoever had been climbing down on it had had a fall. The doctor, who was tall, leaned out as far as he could with his lamp over the empty space. He estimated that this third abyss was about thirty to forty feet deep, ending in a subterranean river.

In great haste they took out the longest rope they had brought with them and fixed it firmly in place of the other. Then the doctor, leaning out again as far as he dared, announced that it was dangling on the stones at the side of the river. Their next descent brought them beside the stream. Traces left on the rocky wall, about the height of a man, made it evident that at times, perhaps when the snow melted, the river rose considerably. Just now, however, the water was not very deep, and its rocky bed could clearly be seen.

Although they were now more than ninety feet down, the policeman noted with relief that the minute speck of light above them could still be seen. They flashed their lamps in all directions, but nothing out of the ordinary was revealed. The river went on underground, and they decided to follow it for a while.

Vincent went first, just in front of Gilles. They had gone about sixty feet when the roof grew so low that they had to proceed on all fours at the edge of the icy water to continue their exploration. Vincent grew increasingly anxious, and the remarks of the policeman, still grumbling to himself in the rear, did nothing to en-

courage him. It was certainly queer that the man hadn't been found at the foot of the rope, for surely he must have injured himself when he fell fifteen or sixteen feet?

At that moment Gilles, who happened to be just ahead of his friend, suddenly stopped.

"Vincent! . . . Look over there!"

Their lamps swung together. The circle of light fell upon the body of a man stretched out on a flat rock eight or nine feet above the river. Vincent and Gilles stood still, shivering.

"Let me pass," the doctor said quickly.

They drew aside to let him and the policeman go by, and followed on behind.

"Yes, that's Rapalli all right," said Vincent in a choked voice.

The man was stretched full length on the damp stone. There was no visible wound, no sign of blood, but his mouth was twisted in agony, and he looked as though he were dead. He must somehow have dragged himself painfully along to that raised stone, to make himself safe from any sudden rising of the waters.

Kneeling beside him, the doctor examined him at great length, manipulating his limbs, listening to his breathing, while the others stood round like statues, hardly daring to breathe. At last the doctor lifted his head.

"He's alive. He's still alive."

Vincent sighed with relief, and came nearer, holding on to Gilles's arm.

"Doctor," he whispered, "do you think he . .?"

The doctor pursed his lips.

"I don't know. He's in a very bad way."

He took a syringe from his bag and, rolling up the wounded man's sleeve, gave him an injection in his arm.

"What shall we do?" said the policeman.

"At the moment, simply wait for the injection to take effect. . . . After that, we'll see. In any case, he can't be moved."

Several minutes went by, heavy with foreboding. Vincent never once took his eyes from the bloodless face of the man who had not scrupled to use all his cunning against the innocent Alberto, but who was now nothing more than a pitiful creature in great pain. He wondered desperately whether they had arrived too late, whether Rapalli was going to die and take the secret of the gold cross of Santa Anna with him to his grave.

16

Rapalli's Secret

THE four were still standing beside the wounded man when both Vincent and Gilles started. He had just moved, the slightest possible movement: but he had moved. Was he about to regain consciousness? At last he opened his eyes, lackluster eyes that focused on nothing. Those watching him switched off their lamps so that they wouldn't blind him. The doctor went up to him with the lantern, felt his pulse, and once more manipulated his limbs.

"Where are you hurt?"

Rapalli did not answer, except to indicate his back with his hand. The doctor nodded his head, for he had already suspected the truth: in his fall, Rapalli had broken his back.

The man stared unseeingly about him for some time, then he painfully articulated a few words in Italian:

"*La croce! . . . la croce d'oro.*"

Vincent started. Rapalli was speaking of the gold cross, and the doctor motioned to the boy to come nearer.

"Speak to him. Ask him what he wants to say."

Vincent knelt beside the dying man.

"Where is the cross of Santa Anna?"

Rapalli did not seem to hear: he had closed his eyes again, and Vincent thought it was all over, that he would not speak again. A few moments later, however, the dimmed eyes opened once more, and now there was a faint flicker of life in them.

"Where is the gold cross of Santa Anna?" Vincent asked again.

The man started. He had become suddenly aware that he was no longer alone at the bottom of the abyss, and he looked up at the unknown faces surrounding him. His gaze fell upon Vincent, and his eyes, so vacant a moment before, were filled with a dreadful fear.

Vincent drew back. But the doctor leaned toward him and said in a low voice:

"He won't be conscious much longer. You must find out as much as you can now."

Vincent bent over the man again.

"The gold cross of Santa Anna. . . . What have you done with it?"

Rapalli closed his eyes, as if to blot out the sight of the face that so disturbed him.

"The gold cross!" he murmured. "The gold cross!" In a whisper he added, "Forgive me! Forgive me!"

For a long while he remained motionless.

Then he tried, without success, to lift his head. The doctor took the blanket they had brought, rolled it up, and slid it beneath the injured man's shoulders.

"The gold cross," murmured Rapalli, ". . . Over there . . . over there . . ." He gestured with his hand, but so vaguely they could not tell whether he meant the abyss, or some more distant place.

"Where is it?" Vincent asked again.

Rapalli's head rolled slowly to the right, then to the left.

"Lost!"

There was another long silence. The man was in pain, in spite of the injection, but it was clear that he wanted to speak. He gave them to understand, with a faint gesture, that he wanted his head lifted a little higher, and the doctor raised it at once. Then Rapalli sighed deeply, looked at the faces surrounding him, and fixed his eyes upon Vincent.

"Forgive me . . . forgive me . . . Alberto is innocent . . . I'm going to die, and that is just . . . that is right."

He stopped speaking. After a while he began again, his voice broken.

"Alberto . . . the chapel of Santa Anna . . . the wall that collapsed. . . . He was working . . . I was in the wood, nearby . . . I heard. . . . Then, one day later . . . Oh, forgive me! . . . the cross, in my knapsack . . . Young Deer Pass . . . the snow, the storm . . . injured . . . the knapsack . . . it rolled, it rolled . . . I ask pardon, for this is my punishment."

Spent by the effort he had made, he relapsed into silence; but his confession had made everything clear. Vincent knew now why Rapalli returned at night to the French slopes: he came to look for the lost cross. Injured in the head and the arm during the snowstorm, he had waited until he was fit again. Then he had returned to prowl about the rim of the abyss, and had made the knotted ropes and the iron hooks to help him lower himself into it, each time going further down. What he had said explained also why he feared Vincent, who hindered him in his comings and goings, since the hut on Wolf Ridge was so near the Black Abyss. He must also have realized that Vincent had picked up the rope he had left behind, and that the rope, if Vincent mentioned it to anyone, could betray him. Rapalli had thought of everything, foreseen everything, yet now he lay at the bottom of the abyss with his back broken.

Very much upset, Vincent fixed his eyes upon Rapalli's lips, which were silent now. He forgot both the lengths to which this man had gone, and the crime he had committed. The miserable wretch had confessed, and so he forgave him. But he would not be wholly satisfied until the cross was found. He wondered whether it had really fallen into the Black Abyss, or whether

Rapalli had lost his knapsack during the snow-storm in some other place. It was so easy to confuse distances in the leaden obscurity of a blizzard.

Once more he leaned over the dying man to question him further. There was no reply, and it was doubtful whether Rapalli heard anything anymore.

"You can leave me alone with him," the doctor said in a low voice. "I don't think he will have the strength to speak again. Wouldn't it be better to look for the gold cross while we're still at the bottom of the abyss?"

"Yes, the gold cross," said the policeman. "His confession is enough for the police, of course. All the same, if we could find the cross . . ."

The policeman, Vincent, and Gilles drew away from Rapalli, switched on their electric lamps, and sent brilliant arrows of light in all directions, but without result.

"It seems to me," said the policeman, "that if that man had lost it here, we would have found it already. A cross made of gold is heavy, and it stays where it falls, like a stone. My guess is that he lost his head in the snowstorm, and didn't know where he was or what he was do-ing."

Both Gilles and Vincent were afraid that that was what had happened. Vincent, however, be-gan thinking on other lines. The river must have risen considerably after the blizzard and the melting of the snows. And even if the gold cross were heavy, heavier than a stone, it was not by itself, but in a knapsack, probably wrapped in paper, and surrounded by other lighter objects. The knapsack might well have been carried along by the rushing waters, and dragged a long way.

He set out along the subterranean river edged by stones and gravel deposited by the water. The roof soon dropped so low that it became impossible to continue the explorations without walking into the stream.

The policeman couldn't believe his eyes: "You don't mean you're going to . . . ?"

"Yes," said Vincent sharply. "I've got to."

The policeman watched the two friends plunge into the icy water up to their knees, and decided not to follow them. Vincent and Gilles went forward for about twenty yards or so, and then the roof came down so low that it was only a short distance above the level of the stream.

"Oh well," said Gilles. "Here goes!"

They continued their exhausting trek through the icy water until they came to another grotto, where the subterranean river widened into a small lake. It was then that Gilles nearly plunged in headlong, crying out as he did so. Vincent only just had time to catch hold of him. The river probably ran into and filled a deep hole at that point, for the light from their lamps could not penetrate the water.

It seemed to Vincent that if Rapalli's knapsack had been swept along by the underground river, it must now be at the bottom of this hole. He unwound Rapalli's rope—which he had brought as a precaution, coiled around his body —and let it fall into the water to measure its depth. Weighted by the iron hook at the end, it went down to the ninth knot before it stopped.

Then the two friends set to work to drag the bottom, using the hook on the rope as a gaff. They threw the rope ten times, twenty times. All at once Gilles cried out that he had felt something on the hook. Pulling on the rope with all their strength, they watched the knots reappearing one by one, and then a dark shape coming to the surface. Vincent rushed to get hold of it, a rucksack already half-rotted by the water. He hastily clutched it to him so that it would not tear and let its contents fall.

"The cross!"

There it was, the cross of Santa Anna. Rapalli must have cleaned all the old paint off before he took it away, and the long spell in the water had in no way damaged the precious metal, which gleamed golden in the light of their lamps.

"The gold cross of Santa Anna," Vincent said again. "Now at last, and only now, Alberto and Rosalba are truly in the clear."

Wildly excited, they went back the way they had come, still wading through the water, and not even aware that they were shivering with cold. They were about to rejoin the doctor and the policeman when they came to a sudden halt. The two men were standing beside Rapalli's recumbent body, and the blanket which the doctor had slipped beneath the injured man's head now covered him completely. Both boys understood what that meant.

"He has just died," the doctor said quietly.

Vincent, very pale, bowed his head as a sign of forgiveness for the unhappy man who had done so much harm.

It only remained now to decide how to bring Rapalli to the surface, a task at once delicate and macabre. As the policeman was roping the body, the doctor came over to Gilles and Vincent and said:

"My dear boys, you've brought off a very fine piece of work. Without you two, that unfortunate wretch would have remained with his secret at the bottom of this abyss for all time, and another man would have carried the burden of a false accusation for the rest of his life."

Placing a hand on their shoulders, he added:

"We've no further need of you just now. You're shivering with cold, you'd better climb up. . . . Besides, there's someone waiting impatiently for you at the hut."

"No," Gilles said quickly, "I want to help. I don't feel cold now."

Vincent felt that he ought to stay too, but Rosalba was all alone on Wolf Ridge, and he couldn't wait to tell her the wonderful news.

Sensing his hesitation, Gilles urged him on: "Yes, Vincent, do go—Rosalba will be so anxious to have word."

So Vincent shook his friend's hand and set off, after one last look at Rapalli, whom they were now ready to bring up. The gold cross was in Vincent's knapsack, strapped securely to his back.

When at last he reached the surface again, darkness had long since fallen upon the mountains. The policeman who had remained at the top was lying wrapped in a blanket, apparently asleep. Vincent didn't stop to wake him. He hurtled down among the rocks with the precious gold cross as though it were he who had stolen it.

This time it was neither fear nor exhaustion that robbed Vincent's legs of their strength, but a wild exultation. He could still hardly believe that the shining proof of Alberto's innocence had been found. Alberto and Rosalba were free to return to Argentera, their mother would join them there, and they would take up their placid life again in the house with the red shutters. He did not feel proud of himself, just immensely happy, and this happiness was so strong that now and again his heart leaped in his breast as though it were going to burst.

Breathless, panting, he came to Wolf Ridge. Shutters and door were carefully closed, but light filtered through the cracks. No need to call out: Miski had recognized his master's step, and set up a joyous barking within.

"Nothing to be afraid of, Rosalba! Open up!"

The door half opened, and Rosalba cried out in fear when she saw Vincent's extraordinary expression, his clothes dripping wet and sticky with mud. For a moment she and Vincent stood staring at each other as if they were paralyzed. Then he took hold of her hands, and squeezed them hard.

"Oh, Vincent, tell me quickly!"

"Rosalba, it's all over! It's all over!"

She wondered what she was supposed to understand by that as she watched Vincent unfastening his knapsack. He took from it the gold cross of Santa Anna, and placed it on the table. Rosalba stared for a moment at the pure gold gleaming beneath the lamp, then she grew pale, and running to Vincent, gave him a hug.

"Rosalba, Alberto is cleared. Rapalli confessed everything before he died at the bottom of the abyss."

"Cleared!" repeated the girl. "My brother is cleared!"

For a long while they said nothing, overwhelmed by such happiness that it was almost too great to be endured.

"Oh, Vincent, now I can go back to Argentera, and find my mother again, and Alberto will come home!"

Then all at once she lifted her head and said anxiously:

"How can we let Alberto know? How can we

tell him? We don't even know where he is."

"In the letter that he left for me he said that he would soon come back . . . and anyway, the story of Rapalli and the gold cross will be in all the papers tomorrow. Alberto's sure to see it. Don't worry, Rosalba. We'll just have to be patient a little while longer, that's all."

Reassured by his words, Rosalba went back to the table where the gold cross was lying. She ran her fingers lightly over the metal and said softly, "We've been saved through your friendship, Vincent."

She could not have expressed a simple truth more perfectly. But in that moment, Vincent did not see himself as a hero. His joy was honest and unalloyed, asking for no reward. . . . Well, yes, perhaps he did hope for one, to match his joy. He hoped that later on, when Alberto had returned and life in a certain house with red shutters had resumed its normal placid course, Rosalba would lean out of her window sometimes and look toward Young Deer Pass and say: "I've a friend over there . . . He's called Vincent . . . He'll be coming to see me again as soon as the snows have melted."

That was all he wanted. That would be the finest possible reward.